THE TOMORROW ARMY

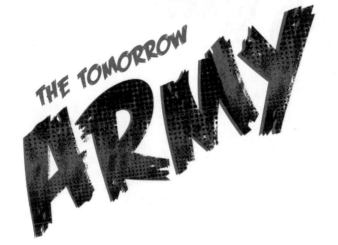

THE TOMORROW ARMY

ABDOPUBLISHING.COM

Reinforced library bound edition published in 2017 by Spotlight, a division of ABDO PO Box 398166, Minneapolis, Minnesota 55439. Spotlight produces high-quality reinforced library bound editions for schools and libraries. Published by agreement with Marvel Press, an imprint of Disney Book Group.

Printed in the United States of America, North Mankato, Minnesota.
042016　092016

♻ THIS BOOK CONTAINS
RECYCLED MATERIALS

MARVEL
marvelkids.com

PUBLISHER'S CATALOGING IN PUBLICATION DATA

Names: Siglain, Michael, author. | Lim, Ron ; Troy, Andy, illustrators.
Title: Captain America : the tomorrow army / by Michael Siglain ; illustrated by Ron Lim and Andy Troy.
Description: Minneapolis, MN : Spotlight, [2017] | Series: Mighty Marvel chapter books
Summary: When S.H.I.E.L.D. learns HYDRA agents are on the rise, Captain America and friends are called on to put an end to HYDRA's evil plans.
Identifiers: LCCN 2016932734 | ISBN 9781614794806 (lib. bdg.)
Subjects: LCSH: Captain America (Fictitious character)--Juvenile fiction. | Avengers (Fictitious characters)--Juvenile fiction. | Superheroes--Juvenile fiction.
Classification: DDC [Fic]--dc23
LC record available at http://lccn.loc.gov/2016932734

Spotlight

A Division of ABDO
abdopublishing.com

STARRING

CAPTAIN
AMERICA

BY **MICHAEL SIGLAIN**

ILLUSTRATED BY

RON LIM AND **ANDY TROY**

MARVEL

Los Angeles
New York

FEATURING YOUR FAVORITES!

The First Avenger!

CAPTAIN AMERICA

Alias

STEVE ROGERS

FALCON

COULSON

Director of S.H.I.E.L.D.

NICK FURY

BLACK WIDOW

IRON MAN

Alias

TONY STARK

ARNIM ZOLA

HYDRA-PRIME

HYDRA

I love New York!

STATUE OF LIBERTY

Steve's coffee guy

CUP OF JOE

OLD JOE

Made of vibranium!

COOL MOTORCYCLE

CAP'S SHIELD

THE STORY OF CAPTAIN AMERICA

*A*ll Steve Rogers ever wanted was to join the army. But he was frail and weak and unable to enlist. Then Steve was chosen to take part in a top secret experiment called **Project: Rebirth.** He was given the Super-Soldier Serum and was bathed in pulsating Vita-Rays.

When the experiment was over, Steve had been transformed from a small and thin weakling into a big, tall, and strong Super-Soldier.

Steve was given a special uniform and an unbreakable red, white, and blue shield made from a rare metal called vibranium. He promised to fight for freedom and equality for all as

CAPTAIN AMERICA!

After one particularly tough battle with the evil villain called Red Skull, Cap's plane crashed into the icy waters of the Arctic. The plane—with Cap still inside—was frozen for many decades, until it was discovered by S.H.I.E.L.D., the world's best super spies. They soon revived Captain America from his icy slumber.

Steve joined S.H.I.E.L.D.'s team of Super Heroes, known as the Avengers. Now, fighting alongside Iron Man, Hulk, Black Widow, Hawkeye, and Falcon, Captain America once again defends liberty and justice from evildoers everywhere!

CHAPTER 1

Steve Rogers woke up at 4:55 a.m., minutes before his alarm clock rang. He jumped out of bed, stretched, and began his morning routine. By 5:15, Steve had already done 3,250 push-ups and 4,500 sit-ups, and he hadn't *even broken a sweat.*

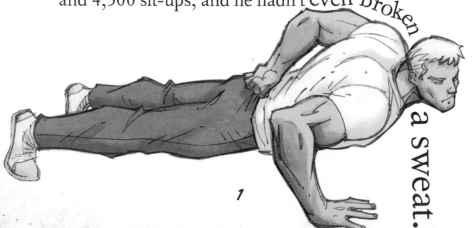

Next it was time for his morning jog—a quick ten-mile run around the streets of **NEW YORK CITY**.

Steve left his apartment, breathed in the warm June air, and began his jog. Good runners could finish a mile in five minutes, Steve could do it in under two.

Steve made his way downtown and to Forty-Second Street, then cut over to Broadway. As he ran, Steve looked up at the giant billboards and bright lights of Times Square. Steve definitely preferred the old Big Apple.

Steve ended his run downtown in front of a newsstand and was instantly greeted with a **"HIYA, CAP"** from the guy working the stand, whom everyone called Old Joe.

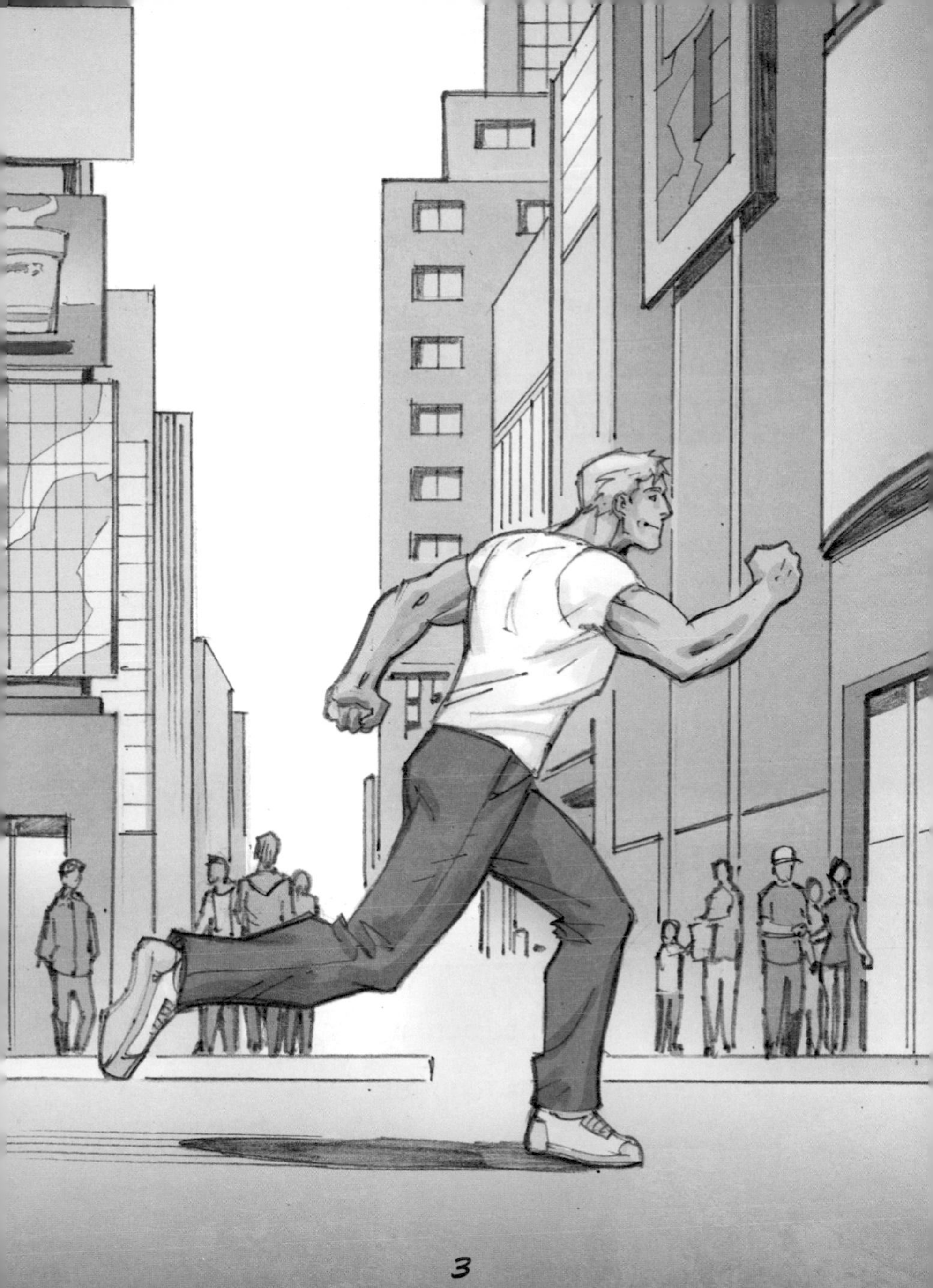

"JUST STEVE, PLEASE," Steve said.

"The usual?" Old Joe called out. Steve nodded, and the man handed him the **DAILY BUGLE**. Steve still couldn't believe a newspaper cost a dollar. He remembered when they were just five cents!

"Glad you're still buying the paper," Old Joe began. "You're my best customer. Most people today get their news from phones or computers. You even pay with actual money. It's like the 1940s all over again," he said with a smile.

Steve smiled back, took the paper, and walked across the street to get a cup of coffee. Usually, he'd go to the local **DINER**.

But after hearing Old Joe talk about the '40s and how different things were today, Steve thought he would try something new, so he made his way to the trendy coffee shop down the block.

The shop was buzzing with people. They barely stopped moving long enough to order their drinks, all of which sounded weird to Steve. He stared at the chalkboard menu.

When it was his turn, Steve asked for "just a cup of joe," and the kid behind the counter stared back at him blankly.

"You want what?" the server asked, confused.

"A CUP OF JOE, BLACK," Steve replied, but there was still no response. "You do sell coffee here, right?" Steve asked. The kid was amazed that someone wanted just a regular black coffee with nothing else in it. Steve paid for his overpriced drink, then took his paper and sat on a bench outside.

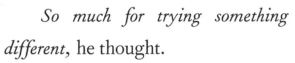

So much for trying something different, he thought.

Steve looked around and sighed. People were walking with their heads down, busy with other things,

oblivious to the world around them. Everyone was connected to technology, but not . . . .
. . . .
. . . .
. . . . to

one another. In Steve's day, people talked to each other. They read and conversed rather than losing themselves in their own virtual worlds.

But before he could continue thinking about how different things were, a strong voice called out to him. **"CAPTAIN, WE HAVE A SITUATION . . ."** the voice began. Steve looked up to see his Avengers teammate Sam Wilson, code name , standing before him. Steve instantly rose to his feet.

"What's the mission?" Steve asked, ready to jump into battle.

IT'S A MATTER OF
**EXTREME
URGENCY!**

Sam began. "I've got an extra ticket to today's Yankees game and no one to go with me. What do you say? Want to take in America's favorite pastime?" he asked.

Steve smiled. It wasn't an actual mission, but a baseball game with Sam would still be fun.

"Count me in," Steve said. "Besides, I haven't been to a ball game since Joltin' Joe played."

"JOLTIN' WHO?" Sam asked as they walked back uptown.

"Never mind," Steve said with a sigh. Little did he know that day would be the start of the most dangerous mission of Cap's career.

CHAPTER 2

Captain America and Falcon stood before Nick Fury, the director of the super-spy group known as S.H.I.E.L.D. Cap—in his **RED**, **WHITE**, and **BLUE** uniform—was a very impressive figure. Next to him was Falcon, wearing a high-tech flight suit that, when activated, allowed him to **FLY** with holographic wings. Both heroes stood at attention on board S.H.I.E.L.D.'s massive

Helicarrier—part aircraft carrier, part heli-
copter, and all state of the art. The ability of
this futuristic vessel to fly unseen above
Manhattan still impressed Steve.

"Gentlemen," the eye-patch-wearing Fury
began as he called up a digital HUD. "Within the
last three weeks, reports of missing persons
around the tristate area have more than
tripled. Men and women, all between
the ages of eighteen and thirty, all
seemingly in perfect health
and in top physical
condition."

"Think they're
all connected?"
Cap asked.

LOCAL LAW
ENFORCEMENT
DOESN'T, BUT
I DO.

"Stay Alert" Fury said. "The kidnappings seem to be random, but **S.H.I.E.L.D.** intelligence tells me that there's something bigger going on. I have several agents hard at work trying to figure out who is behind this, and why."

"What's our involvement?" Falcon asked.

"Right now, observe and report only. I want you up to speed for when we need to act," Fury said.

As Cap and Falcon walked out of Fury's office, the First Avenger felt disappointed.

He was looking forward to some action, not sitting on the sidelines. But before he could harp

on the issue too long, Falcon gave him a nudge.

"Come on, Cap," Falcon said. "We're going to be late for the game. The Helicarrier is going up the East Coast and will be over the Bronx in two minutes—just enough time for us to change into less conspicuous clothing."

Steve Rogers walked around Yankee Stadium in shock. There was music blasting, a huge TV, dozens of smaller TVs, various fancy restaurants and food stands, and even clothing shops.

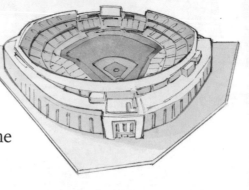

"This certainly isn't the House that Ruth Built," he said to Sam.

"You're living in another time, man. Welcome to the twenty-first century, where everything is at your fingertips!" Sam said.

As they sat, Steve wondered why a music video kept playing on the jumbotron screen. "Oh, that's one of the outfielders," Sam said. "He has the number-three song in the country."

"Babe Ruth and Joe DiMaggio never sang," Steve said under his breath. "Isn't anyone interested in the game anymore?"

But before Sam could respond, their

S.H.I.E.L.D. emergency beacons started to **BLINK**. It was Fury. There was a team of college kids on the way to the game, but their bus had gone missing. S.H.I.E.L.D. intercepted the garbled 911 call, and Sam and Steve were being called in to respond.

They ran out of the stadium and stood before Steve's **vintage 1942 Harley-Davidson motorcycle.** "You can't be serious," Sam said, referring to the battered and bruised cycle. "You could walk faster than that thing goes." But Steve was already opening a large duffel bag to reveal his Captain America uniform and vibranium shield.

"She hasn't failed me yet," Cap said with a smile. "Now suit up and hop on."

"No way. I can fly. I'll carry you," Sam responded as his holographic hard-light wings began to form.

"Not a chance," Steve said as he lowered his mask into position. He jumped on his bike and started it with a loud roar. **Now THIS was Cap's favorite pastime!**

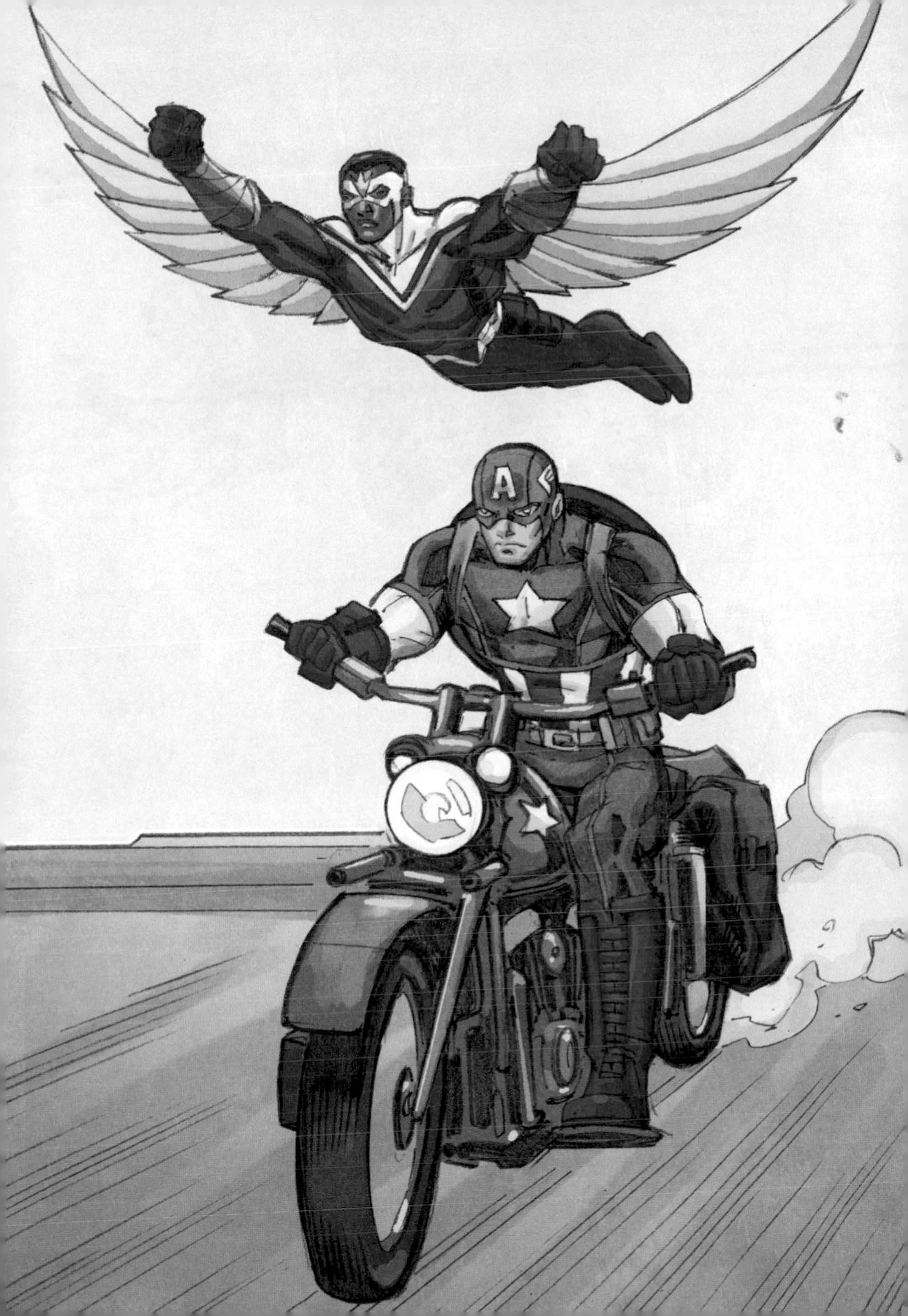

CHAPTER 3

*F*alcon shook his head, then took to the air and activated the GPS on his watch. "I've got a lock on them, so try to keep up!" Falcon said as he flew toward the Major Deegan Expressway. Captain America followed on his bike, darting *IN* and *OUT* of traffic until he spotted the hijacked school bus.

Cap sped past all the other cars until he was

right behind the bus. Suddenly, the emergency doors at the back of the bus burst open.

Energy beams shot from the windows. Whoever these guys were, they were very heavily armed.

FALCON! I COULD USE A DIVERSION!

"UNDERSTOOD,"

Falcon said. The flying hero dove down and fired a grappling hook at the roof of the bus, penetrating the thick top. Falcon swung high into the air and yanked with all his might, causing the driver to swerve. The distraction worked! Cap sped up and drove out of harm's way.

Inside the bus, an armed goon attached a small device to the end of the grappling hook and sent an electric charge up the wire and straight back to Falcon. It **SHOCKED** the hero, and Falcon fell to the ground. The villain laughed as the bus sped away. "We did it," the goon said. "Inform headquarters that the test subjects will be there within the hour."

The Goon

But before the driver could respond, he pointed out the window; the armed goon followed his gaze. "No! It can't be," the driver said in disbelief. The villains saw him from a distance, standing atop an overpass, looking directly at them: it was Captain America!

Cap jumped on his bike and revved the engine, but it sputtered out. "Not now!" Cap said under his breath. He tried his bike again.

Nothing!

The bus was getting closer and closer. He tried a third time. The bike sputtered again and then conked out.

The motorcycle that had never failed. . . failed. By then the bus was almost under the overpass. There was only one thing to do. Captain America ran at full speed and

JUMPED!

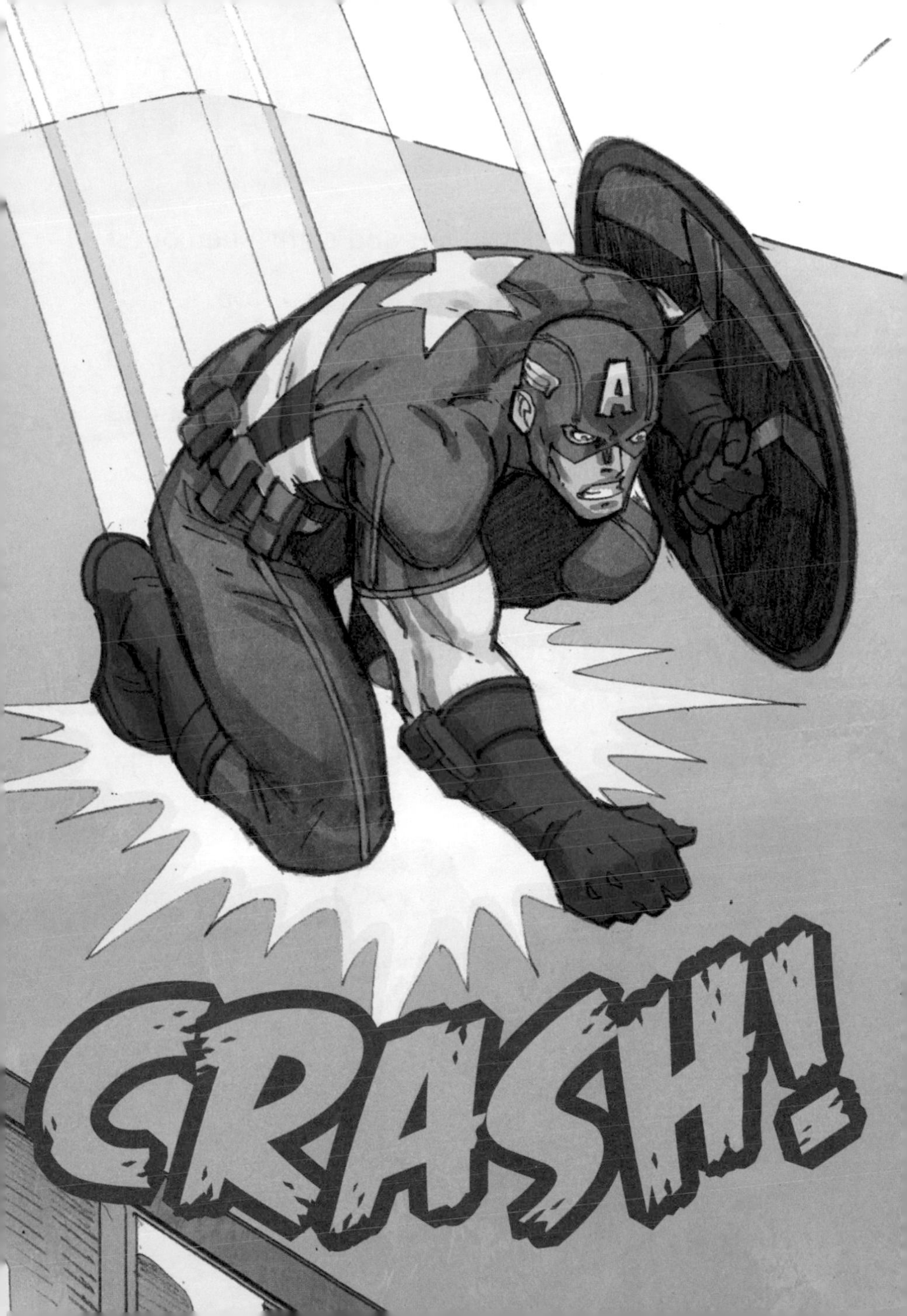
CRASH!

The bus swerved left and right, then burst through a guardrail and came to a stop.

Cap, who had been clinging to the top of the bus, quickly jumped to his feet and swung down through one of the side windows.

"Ah, the great Captain America," the villain said as he raised his weapon.

The goon fired, but Cap was too fast. The beams **bounced** off his raised shield. Then Cap *THREW* his shield! The

DOOM!"

hostages stood there, stunned, as the goon fell to the ground. Then Cap noticed that the driver had gotten away.

"Wait here," he instructed the hostages. "I'll be right back!"

Captain America jumped off the bus and ran at top speed toward the driver. The driver had pulled out a high-tech energy weapon, ready to fire, when—

WHAM!

Falcon smashed down on the villain and **KNOCKED HIM OUT COLD.**

"Who are these guys?" Falcon asked.

"I don't know, but they're too heavily armed for a hostage situation," Cap said. "Fury's right: there's more to this than meets the eye. And I don't like it."

"Captain America? Falcon?" a voice called from behind them. "We'll take it from here." It was Agent Coulson from **S.H.I.E.L.D.** He and his team were ushering the hostages off the bus and taking the villains into custody. "Please report to Director Fury's office at oh seven hundred tomorrow morning," Coulson said. Then he wheeled Cap's bike up to him. "Think you might want to requisition a new ride, Captain," Coulson quipped.

"No, thanks," Cap said as he quickly took the bike from him and wheeled it off toward the **S.H.I.E.L.D.** trucks.

"Was it something I said?" Coulson asked Falcon.

"Nah, he's just upset. He almost jeopardized the hostages thanks to his old motorcycle."

Cap heard what Falcon said. **And he was right.**

CHAPTER 4

At seven the next morning, Steve Rogers stood in his civilian clothing before Director Fury.

THANKS FOR COMING IN, CAP. PLEASE SIT DOWN. SAM WILL JOIN US LATER. FIRST, WE NEED TO TALK.

YOU WERE RIGHT. THAT WASN'T A NORMAL KIDNAPPING ATTEMPT.

"Coulson will deal with what happened yesterday," Fury said before changing the subject. "Your help is needed elsewhere." He pressed a button under his desk.

The windows went black as a flat-screen TV lowered itself from the ceiling. "Watch this, and then we'll talk," Fury said as he pressed another button.

Steve watched the screen as the men in the video spoke in hushed tones. "Notice anything special about those men?" Fury asked. Steve studied the video more closely.

"There are six of them, but . . . but only two of them look . . . real," Steve said, almost in disbelief.

"Good eye. The other four are advanced holograms. But keep watching." Fury said.

"EVERYTHING IS PROCEEDING ACCORD-
ING TO SCHEDULE. THE TECHNO-DISRUPTOR
HAS BEEN COMPLETED AND THE TOMORROW
ARMY WILL SOON BE READY," said one of the
holograms.

"EXCELLENT. THE FINAL MEETING IS SET
FOR MIDNIGHT TOMORROW AT GRAVESEND
BAY," said one of the non-holograms. "I WILL
INFORM OUR LEADER." And with that, the

video abruptly ended and the light in the office returned. Steve turned toward Fury.

"What is the Tomorrow Army?" Steve asked. "And where did this video come from?"

Fury pressed another button; a few seconds later, the beautiful yet dangerous Natasha Romanoff, code name Black Widow, entered the room.

"I took the video, and it wasn't easy," Natasha said, then explained how she'd had to hold herself up in the rafters. "After the video cut out and the holograms disappeared, the two men raised both their arms and said:

HAIL, HYDRA!

Steve's fists clenched at the mere mention of *HYDRA*, an evil organization that wanted to take over the world. They were the very opposite of the super spies who made up **S.H.I.E.L.D.** and worked to keep the world safe.

"I followed them down a hidden elevator shaft and tailed them to a secret underground train- ing room. There were dozens of guards—all training with dif- ferent weapons or in different fighting styles. . .and all wearing *HYDRA* badges," Natasha said.

"It's not possible," Steve said. "*HYDRA* was defeated almost

a century ago—by me!"
"That's what we thought,"
Fury said. "Then we
found this."

He handed Cap an *envelope marked*
TOP SECRET. "Twelve of my best
agents ended up in the hospital getting us this
info," Fury said. Cap opened the envelope to
find several glossy pictures. "I think you'll
recognize the person in the center of the room."

Steve's eyes widened, and his blood ran
COLD. "No . . ." Steve whispered. The figure in the picture was a hulking one. It had a
large half-human, half-robotic body—but its
face wasn't on its head. Instead, it was on a tele-
vision-like flat screen in the center of its body.
The body was unrecognizable, but the face

was unmistakable. It was **HYDRA** scientist
and second-in-command Arnim Zola. Like
Steve, Zola had fought in World War II. But
Steve had thought Zola long dead.

In the photos, Zola was standing in front
of a high-tech machine straight out of
a science-fiction movie. "Somehow, Arnim
Zola survived all these years and is now the
head of Hydra," Fury said. "We believe that
the thing he's standing in front of is the Techno-
Disruptor." Then Fury turned to face Steve,
who had already suited up and was ready for
battle.

When Cap went to grab his shield, he noticed a new black-and-gray uniform that hung next to it. "That's your new stealth suit," a voice behind him said. It was Nick Fury again. "It will allow you to sneak into the **HYDRA** meeting place without being detected," the director said. "It's a present from Tony Stark. He's making them for all the **AVENGERS**.

"I know you prefer **red, white,** and **blue**—but this will keep you from being caught and becoming **black** and **blue**," Fury said with a grin.

As Fury left, Cap suited up again and made his way into **S.H.I.E.L.D.'s** equipment room.

Agent Coulson approached Cap with Cap's bike. "You know, we can add a rocket launcher, a GPS, even a cup holder to this thing," Coulson began, but Cap refused. This was

WHOOSH!

a classic bike, after all, and he didn't want to change it. "I once felt the same way about Lola," Coulson said as he got into his classic red Corvette.

He flipped a switch. And with that, Coulson and Lola rocketed toward New York City below.

Cap shook his head at the flying car as Falcon and Black Widow stepped up behind him.

"I just heard the news about HYDRA," Sam said. "When do we go after them?"

"We don't. I do," Cap replied.

"Let me help!" Sam responded. But Cap refused. He was going in solo to find out more about HYDRA'S secret plans, and he didn't need help. HYDRA was a dangerous and evil organization from Steve's past, and he knew exactly how to handle it.

But Cap wanted to be extra careful, especially when it came to his friends.

Sam walked off, frustrated that he couldn't help, but Natasha stayed behind to have a word with Steve.

SPYING ON HYDRA ALONE, AND ON THIS RICKETY OLD BIKE, REALLY ISN'T SMART. I SHOULD DO THIS MISSION.

I'VE GOT THE SITUATION UNDER CONTROL.

I'M SURE YOU DO—BUT TAKE THIS WITH YOU.

It was an emergency signal. If Cap was overwhelmed, he'd tap the screen and **S.H.I.E.L.D.** would be there.

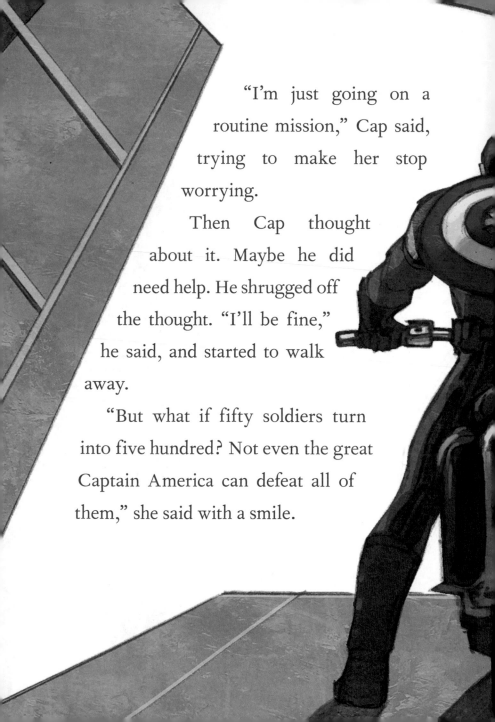

"I'm just going on a routine mission," Cap said, trying to make her stop worrying.

Then Cap thought about it. Maybe he did need help. He shrugged off the thought. "I'll be fine," he said, and started to walk away.

"But what if fifty soldiers turn into five hundred? Not even the great Captain America can defeat all of them," she said with a smile.

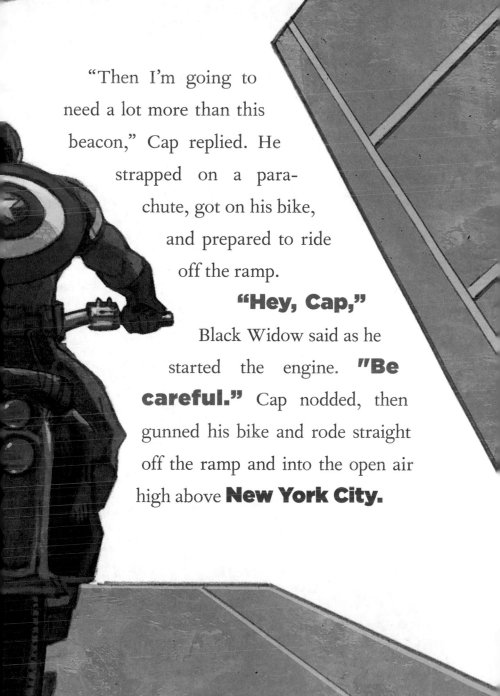

"Then I'm going to need a lot more than this beacon," Cap replied. He strapped on a parachute, got on his bike, and prepared to ride off the ramp. **"Hey, Cap,"** Black Widow said as he started the engine. **"Be careful."** Cap nodded, then gunned his bike and rode straight off the ramp and into the open air high above **New York City.**

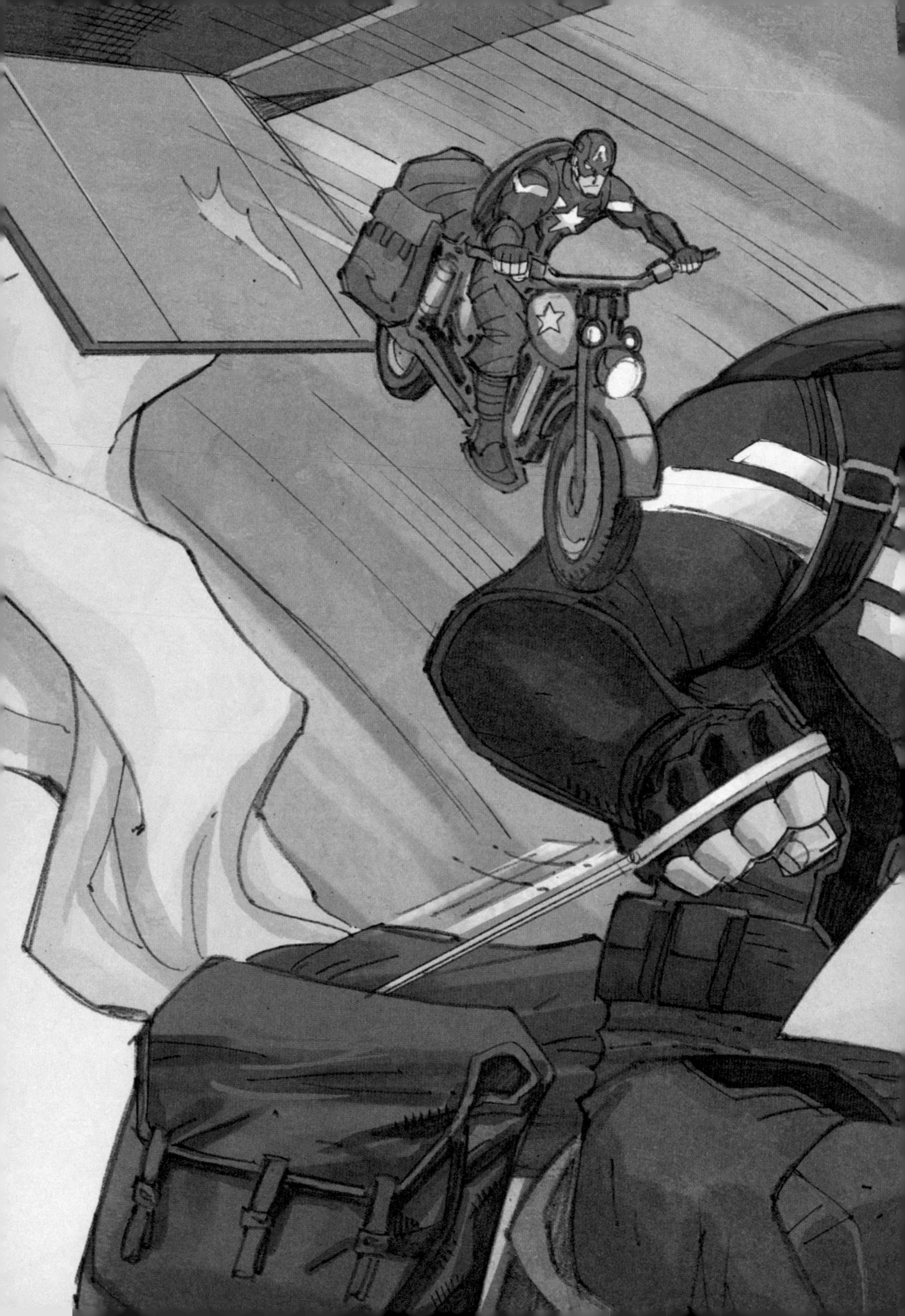

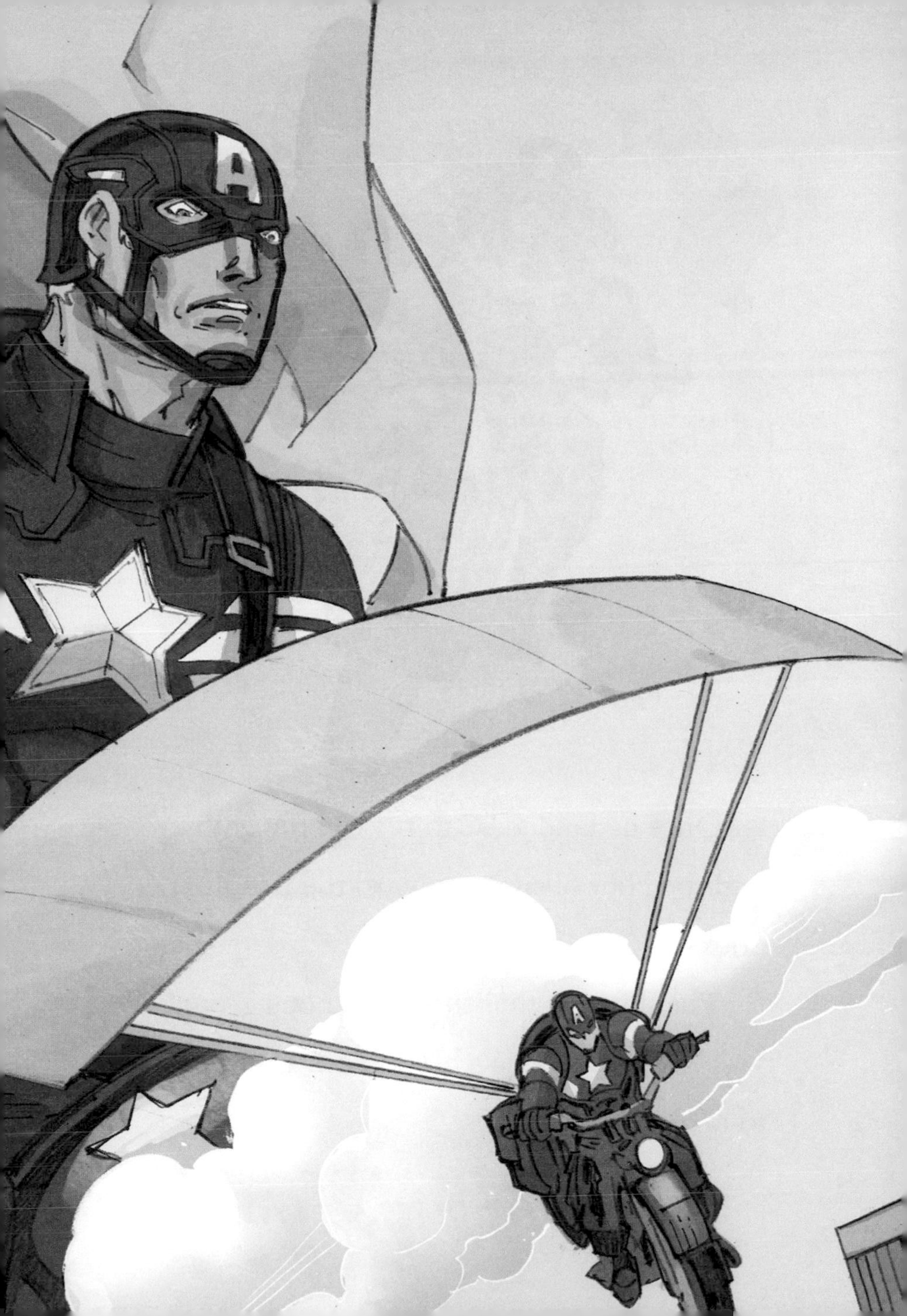

Once he landed, Cap revved the engine and sped out of sight, toward the Brooklyn docks.

The thought that this venomous group was back made Cap's blood boil. It was time to take the fight to

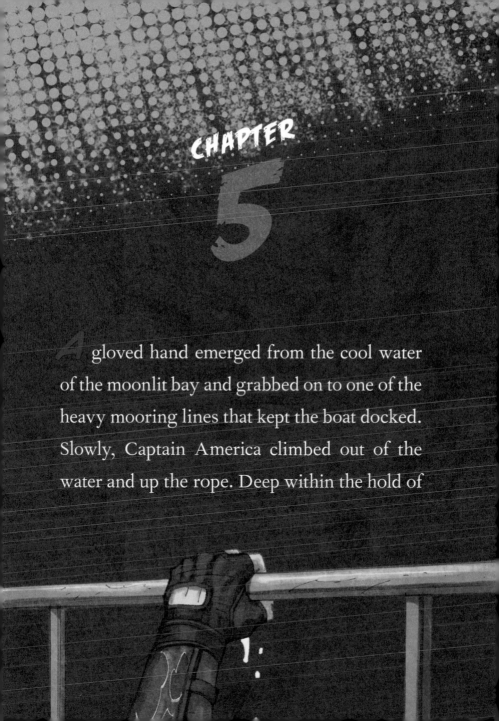

CHAPTER 5

A gloved hand emerged from the cool water of the moonlit bay and grabbed on to one of the heavy mooring lines that kept the boat docked. Slowly, Captain America climbed out of the water and up the rope. Deep within the hold of the boat was a high-tech **HYDRA** meeting room, and Cap was going to find it.

He quietly made his way across the deck, taking out one **HYDRA** guard after another.

Cap's new uniform was a great help. The black-and-gray suit allowed him to blend with shadows and move without being seen.

Cap quickly took out a big guard with his trusty shield. He left the unconscious guard locked in a storage room but without his helmet and armor. Cap, now disguised as a

HYDRA guard, made his way to the bottom of the boat and into the secret meeting room. He stood silently in the back. At the center of the room was something—or someone. It was standing upright and was surrounded by a dozen **HYDRA** scientists, all of whom had evil smiles on their evil faces. They spoke of special gauntlets and boots that could increase

a man's **STRENGTH** and *SPEED*;
of high-tech armor and state-of-the-art helmets—helmets that were combat ready and could withstand a blast at point-blank range. Then they mentioned that this futuristic weaponry was ready to test today. Captain America had heard enough.

"Party's over, boys!" Cap said as he ripped off his *HYDRA* disguise and jumped into the center of the room. The guards fired their weapons immediately, but they were no match for Cap! Captain America raised his shield and blocked every attack, sending bullets and laser beams back toward the *HYDRA* agents, blasting them down and knocking them out.

"You are so right, Captain," one of the

HYDRA scientists began. "But for you!"

The scientist then pressed a code into a keypad, and the metal box in the center of the room began to open with an eerie **HISSS.**

As the box opened, a high-tech **HYDRA** agent stepped out wearing the same devices that the other agents had been speaking about earlier. The super **HYDRA** goon clenched his fists, smirked, and took a step toward Cap.

The super-agent raised his gauntlets and brought them crashing down on Cap with ease. Cap lifted his shield at the last possible second to block the blow, but the shock wave went right through him and rattled his bones. *Wow,* Cap thought. *Felt like Thor bashed me with Mjolnir.* Before Cap knew it, the super-agent was on the

Cap dodged a punch, but then the super-agent grabbed him by the shoulder and unleashed an intense electroshock.

Cap screamed in pain and pushed forward, delivering a massive right hook to the agent's jaw that caused him to release Cap from his grip.

"You have a strong fighting spirit," the super-agent began. "But you are unwise to continue this fight. **You are no match for me,**

"I'VE NEVER RUN FROM A FIGHT, AND I'M NOT ABOUT TO START NOW!"

Cap leaped into the air, but the **HYDRA** super-agent was too fast for him. He reared back and brought his fists **SLAMMING** down on Cap. Cap raised his shield again, but it was no use.

WHOOSH!

Cap landed with a hard **THUD** on the far side of the meeting room and momentarily blacked out. When he opened his eyes, Cap couldn't believe what had happened to his shield.

CAPTAIN AMERICA WAS IN TROUBLE.

He struggled to his feet as the super-agent charged toward him. Cap slowly raised his dented shield. But the super-agent was already looming above him.

The super-agent grabbed Cap's shield and flung it across the room—with Cap attached! Cap landed on his feet and quickly slung his shield across his back.

He moved in close and delivered a series of punches to no avail.

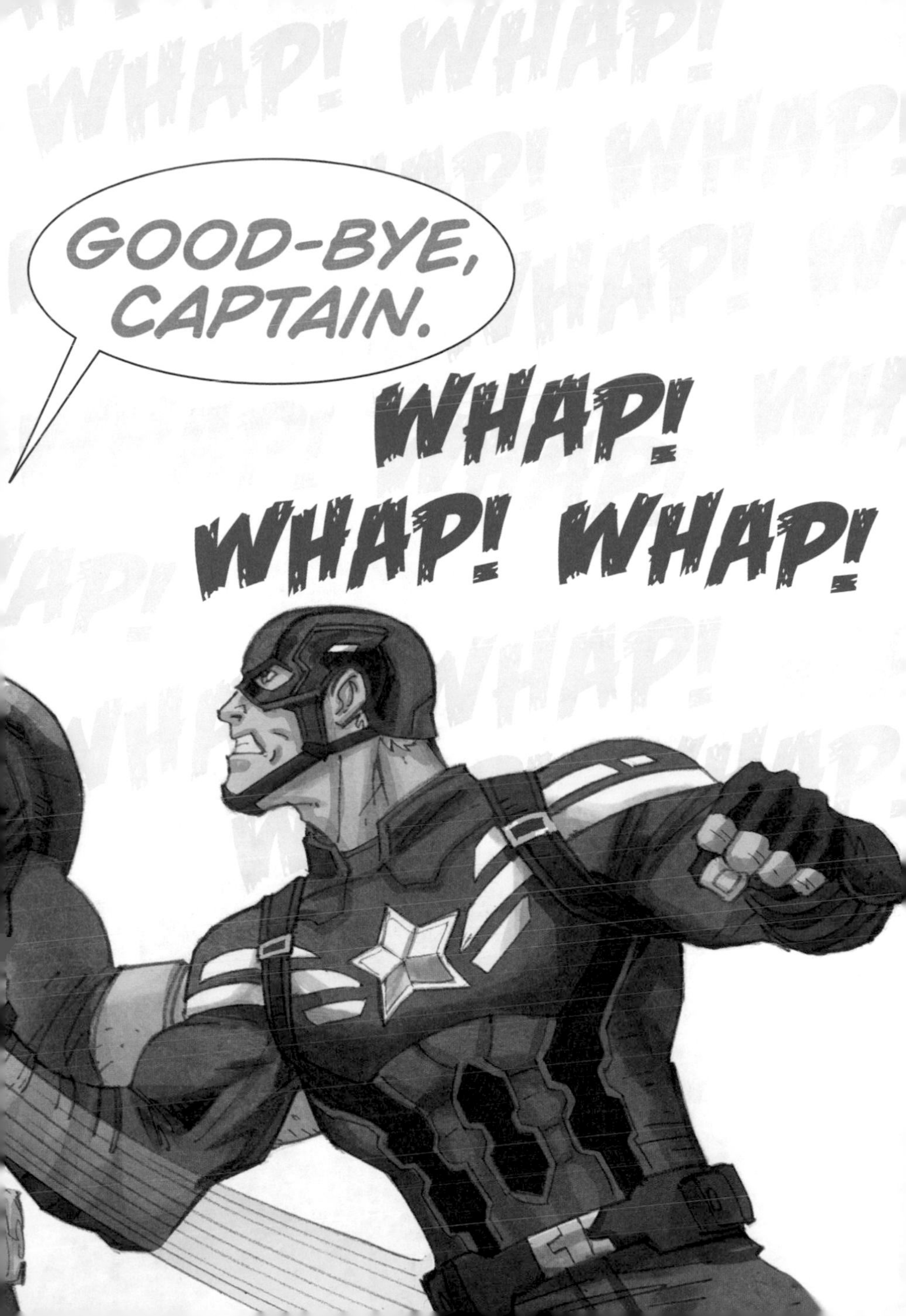
GOOD-BYE, CAPTAIN.
WHAP! WHAP! WHAP!

The super-agent looked down at Cap and grinned.

He then pressed a switch on his gauntlet and began to punch. And he punched and punched and punched—faster and faster and faster.

Then he sent another SHOCK through Cap's body that nearly ZAPPED him right out of his boots.

Cap fell to his knees, barely conscious from the assault. He quickly reached into his pouch and pressed Black Widow's emergency beacon. Just in time, too. The super-agent was moving in for the final, finishing blow when a voice yelled out:

ENOUGH!

A shiver ran down Cap's spine. His vision was blurry, but he could still see the unmistakable form of **Arnim Zola!** The villain from Cap's past—who now looked like something from the future—stood before the fallen First Avenger and spoke. "Good evening, Herr Captain. Welcome aboard."

"**Zola . . .**" Cap hesitated. "You'll never get away with this."

"Ah, ever the optimist," **Zola** said. "But clearly, you are no match for my

TOMORROW ARMY.

This super-agent who bested you is merely the prototype. Soon, there will be dozens more. Hundreds, even! And no one—not you, or **S.H.I.E.L.D.,** or your mighty Avengers— will be able to defeat them. I will do what **RED SKULL** never could—

I, ARNIM ZOLA, WILL RULE THE WORLD!!!"

"**Zola!**" One of the scientists quickly interrupted. "Fighter jets are approaching!"

A battered Cap managed a smile.

"This is inconvenient, but not unexpected," **Zola** replied. He turned to the other scientists. "Evacuate the boat. Then blow it." **Zola** looked at Cap and gave him *one final blow.*

17...16...15

14...13...12

11...10...9...

Cap heard the escape subs shoot out from beneath. He then heard a timer ticking down toward zero. As he struggled to remain conscious, he heard a familiar voice.

WHAT ARE YOU DOING? TAKING A NAP?

8 - - 7 - - 6 - - 5 - -

Falcon was standing before him.

He grabbed Cap and activated his hard-light wings.

The winged Avenger radioed Black Widow, who was watching from the Quinjet high above the boat. **"I've got him,"** Falcon said.

"Well, what are you waiting for? Get to the main deck and get out of there!" Black Widow yelled.

Falcon grabbed Cap and flew high into the sky.

"Get the medical bay ready," Falcon said as they flew away.

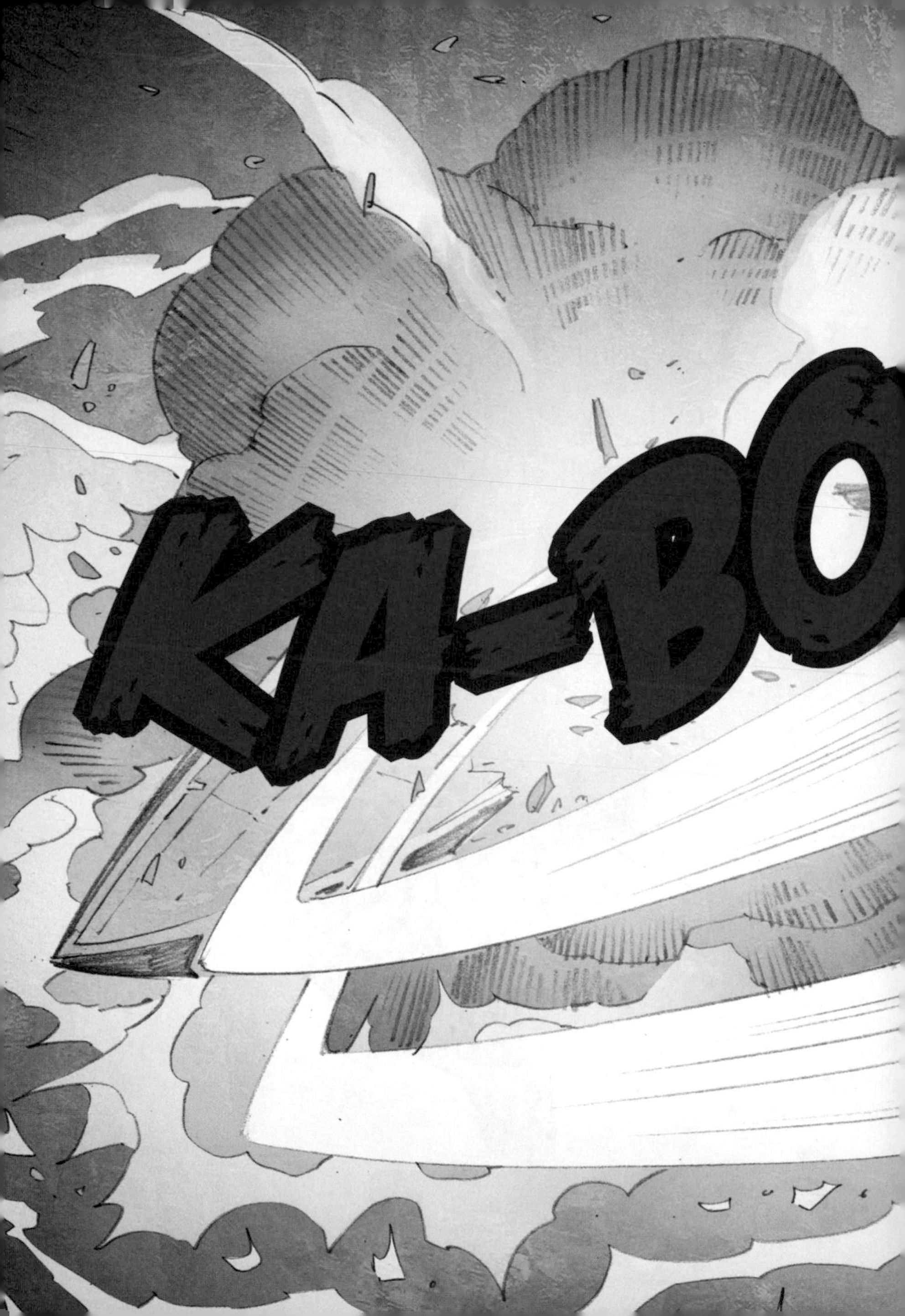
KA-BO

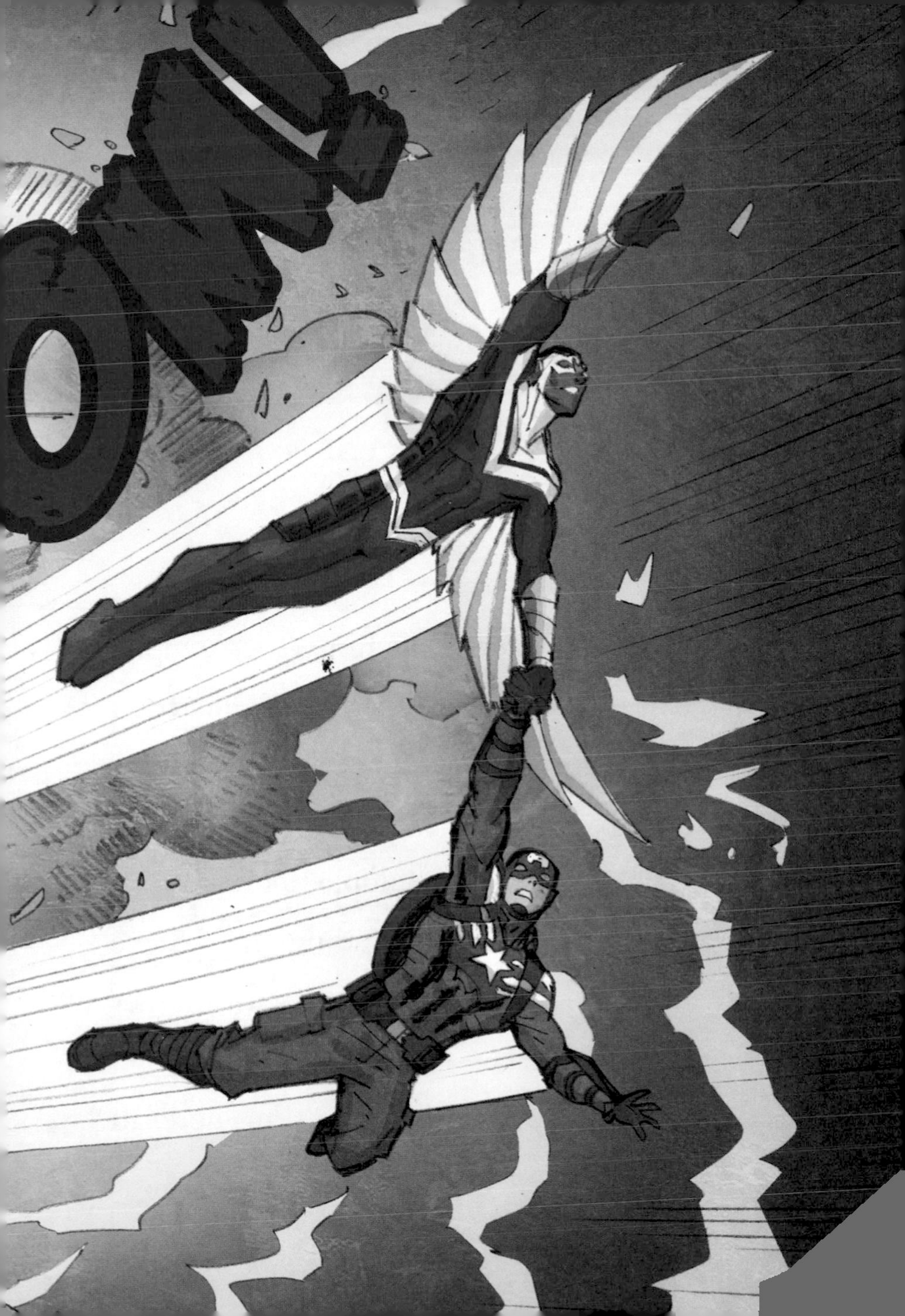

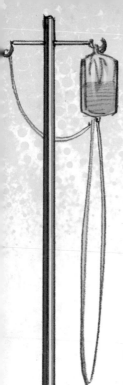

CHAPTER 6

*W*eeks later, Steve Rogers woke up in the medical bay on board the Helicarrier.

"Ugh...what hit me?" he asked.

"A prototype **HYDRA** super-agent," Nick Fury said. "Multiple times."

"Thanks for reminding me," Steve said. "I suppose you're here with another mission?"

"No," Fury began. "I'm here to

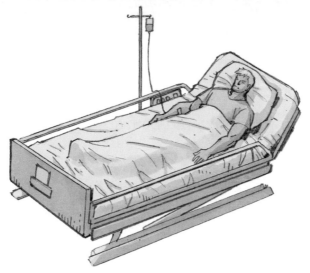

make sure you're all right. You took a bad beating, Captain," he said as he walked over and looked Steve in the eye. "And you used poor judgment. This isn't the same **HYDRA** you fought during World War II. This is a new-and-improved **HYDRA**. They adapted with the times. You didn't. Your mission...was a failure."

Fury's words hurt almost as much as Steve's wounds. *He's right,* Steve thought. Steve had acted alone instead of accepting help. He'd thought his enemies were just like he was and fighting them would be just like it used to be. But he had been wrong.

"Thanks to the Super-Soldier Serum, you're going to be fine. You should be cleared to leave in another week or two."

"A week? Or two? But what about *HYDRA?"* Steve asked.

"We've learned that *HYDRA* is going to make a move in five days—on the *FOURTH OF JULY.* You can watch the events from your hospital bed," Fury said before leaving.

Steve thought long and hard about what Fury had told him. He wasn't about to let Black Widow, Falcon, and the agents of **S.H.I.E.L.D.** go up against Zola and *HYDRA* without him.

But Steve was still uncomfortable in this modern world. He liked the things he knew: the old Times Square, black coffee, his 1942 Harley. If he was going to adjust to the modern world, he would need help, and Steve knew just where to turn. He checked himself out and left to find a friend.

A RED-AND-GOLD BLUR

streaked across the New York skyline and came to a stop atop a glistening state-of-the-art skyscraper. Steve Rogers, with his dented shield slung across his back, walked across the roof and addressed the red-and-gold Super Hero who stood before him.

"**Hello, Tony,**" Steve said to the invincible Iron Man.

"**Oh, hey, Cap,**" Iron Man nonchalantly said as his faceplate lifted to reveal the handsome **Tony Stark.**

"I didn't see you there. **WHAT'S UP?**"

"IS IT AN AVENGERS MISSION?"

"DOES FURY NEED HELP WITH SOMETHING?"

"ALIEN INVASION?"

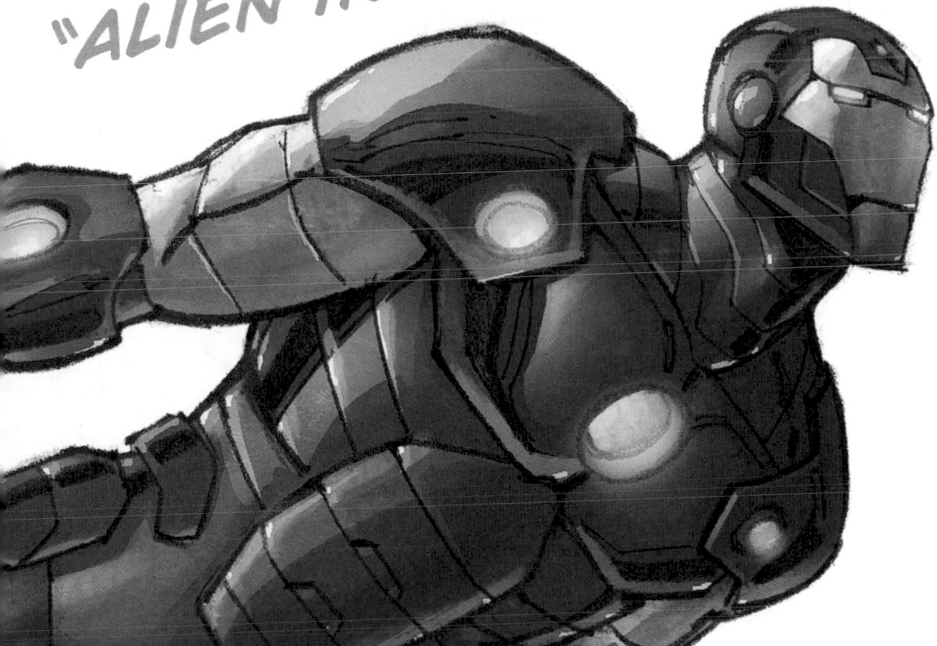

"RAMPAGING ROBOTS?"

"MOLE MEN?"

"SOMETHING STUCK IN HIS GOOD EYE?"

"It's not an Avengers mission, and Fury doesn't need help," Steve said. "I do." Tony's smiling face turned momentarily confused, and then Tony invited his fellow Avenger inside **Stark Tower.**

Steve explained everything that had happened in the past few weeks. No details were left out. When he was done, Tony let out a long sigh.

SO WE'RE DEALING WITH AN ARMY OF HIGH-TECH SUPER VILLAINS LED BY A DUDE OLDER THAN YOU WHOSE FACE IS ON A TV IN HIS BELLY?

"You forgot about the Techno-Disruptor, whatever that is . . ." said Steve.

"Right. It's a device that can knock out and shut down specific technology," Tony said.

Steve was shocked.

"How do you know all that?"

"I'm a genius billionaire inventor. I know everything," Tony said. "Plus, I hacked **S.H.I.E.L.D.'s** encrypted files last night. Anyway, we've got our work cut out for us. But if anyone can bring you into the twenty-first century, it's me."

Tony continued. "Once we do that, then we'll do something about your horribly

outdated wardrobe," Tony added under his breath. "Then you can hit the town and do the **jitterbug** or whatever the craze was a hundred years ago."

Steve stared at his clothes, unsure whether Tony was joking with him or insulting him.

Tony smiled. **"Come on, Cap, let's go!"**

During the next four days, Tony taught Steve everything he could about the modern world.

EIGHT THOUSAND FIVE HUNDRED SIXTY-SEVEN . . .

And all the while, Steve was getting stronger and healthier. Not only was he doing ten thousand sit-ups and push-ups again by the end of day three, he was also texting. Tony Stark was proud, though there was one major upgrade left.

Tony led Steve into a large room that was part garage, part laboratory, and part man cave—but that wasn't what impressed Steve. The room was lined with new Iron Man armors, all in various stages of development. Tony couldn't help noticing Steve's reaction to all the suits.

CAP! CHECK OUT THIS SELFIE!

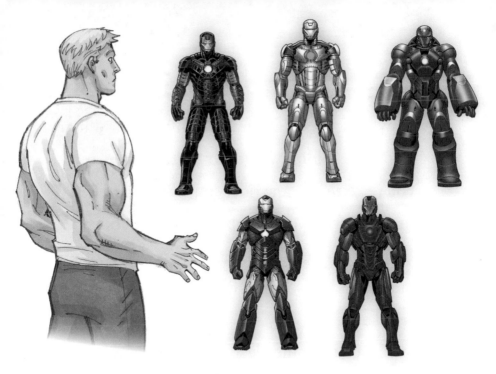

"Cool, right?" Tony remarked. He walked over to Steve's 1942 Harley. "But we're here to discuss this ancient two-wheeled vehicle that may have, at one point, been called a motocycle."

"Look, I've listened to you on everything else. Don't even try to talk me into a new bike!" Steve exclaimed.

"Do. Or do not. There is no try," Tony said, much to Steve's confusion. "What? It's Yoda. Didn't we get to that? Never mind. You're getting a new ride, courtesy of me. Or do you want to have to jump onto another bus?"

Steve looked from his bike to Tony, then back to his bike. "What did you have in mind?" he asked.

A wicked smile flashed across Tony's face. **"Two words,"** he began.

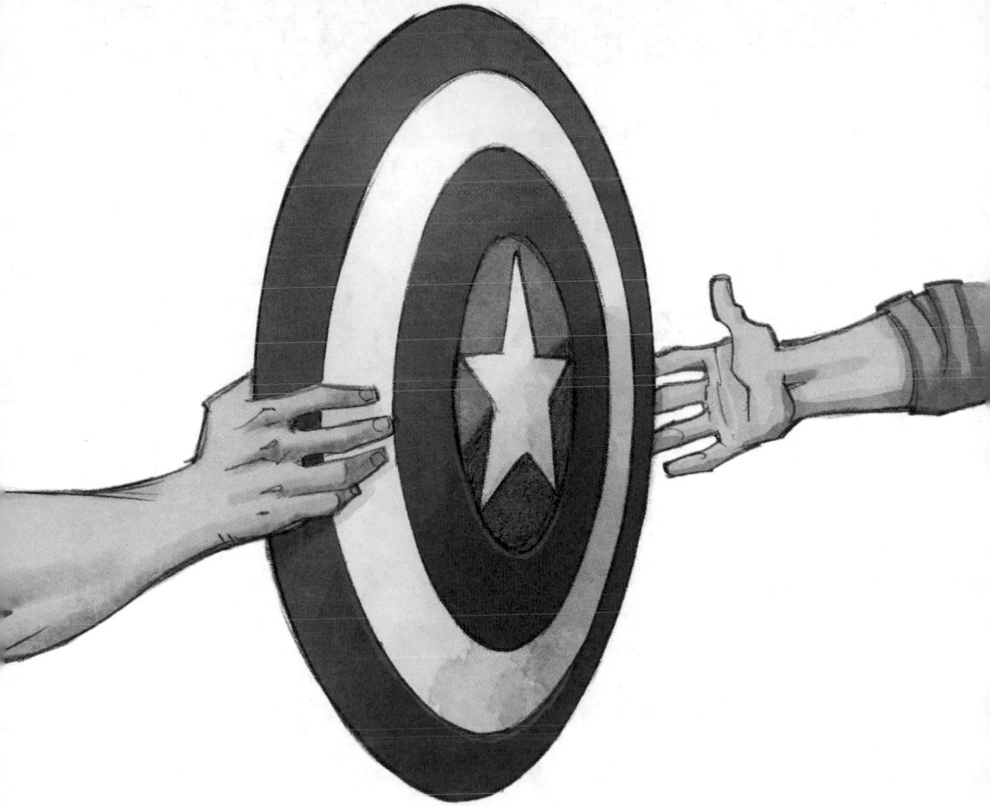

Steve gulped. "All right," he said. "But on one condition: you fix this first."

"My pop made this," Tony said. His father, **Howard Stark,** had crafted Steve's iconic shield. Tony looked at it and understood Steve's connection to the things from his past.

Then that mischievous smile came back to Tony's face. "These little dents? I can bang them out in no time. Then we fix your bike, get you back to the Helicarrier so you can stop **HYDRA,** and still have you home in time to watch the fireworks."

"You want in?" Steve asked. "I could use the armored Avenger when I take on those super-agents."

"Thanks, but I have to be in Europe by midnight. Reports are that Crimson Dynamo has been spotted near Italy—plus, I'd like some gelato for dessert."

And with that, the two heroes got back to work. It was going to be a long night.

CHAPTER

7

*T*he next morning, Captain America found himself again aboard the Helicarrier and inside Nick Fury's office. **"Where have you been, Captain?"** Fury asked, wondering why Steve had checked himself out of the medical bay days earlier.

"I went to see a friend," Steve began. "He helped me get back in the game. I'm ready to take on HYDRA. But I'll need a little help."

"You're America's First Super Soldier and the First Avenger, and it's the Fourth of July," Fury replied as he extended his hand. "You can have all the help you need." The two men shook hands, and it was as if Cap had never left.

"What's the latest intelligence update?" Cap asked.

"Thanks to scraps recovered from the boat and surveillance from our best agents, including Black Widow, we have determined that HYDRA will strike this evening at the very symbol of American freedom: the Statue of Liberty."

"And what, exactly, is Zola's plan?" Cap asked.

> IT'S JUST LIKE HE SAID: HE PLANS TO TAKE OVER THE WORLD WITH HIS TOMORROW ARMY.

"Regular men and women have been turned into an unwitting evil army. Those athletes on the bus—the ones you saved on their way to the Yankees game—they were part of **Zola's** plan. They were his test subjects. **HYDRA'S** been kidnapping people and brainwashing them. **Zola's** been downloading **HYDRA** fighting skills and orders directly into their brains and then hooking them up to all this superior, futuristic tech—making them nearly unstoppable."

"And is each one as strong as the prototype I fought?" Cap asked.

Fury nodded.

"And you're sure of their target?" Cap asked.

"Yes. I believe **Zola** wants to make a very public display," Fury responded.

"Agreed," Cap said. He thought for a moment and then added, "I need a battalion of your best **S.H.I.E.L.D.** agents. Black Widow, Falcon, and I will lead them into battle."

Fury flashed a rare smile, suddenly feeling much more confident.

"I'm not done," Cap said, much to the director's surprise. "I'm also going to need some tech."

Nick Fury raised his unpatched eyebrow.

"Did Captain America just ask for tech?" Fury said.

Later, Agent Coulson led Captain America into the Helicarrier's Research and Development area. Cap made his way to the sonic disruptors and precise EMP blasters. "These are all nonlethal and won't hurt **HYDRA'S** unwitting army, but they should do damage against **Zola's** tech," Cap said, much to Coulson's surprise.

"I'll also need a team of our top programmers to be stationed nearby the fighting so they can work on creating firewalls and jamming frequencies to block **HYDRA'S** intelligence network," Cap added. Agent Coulson was clearly impressed.

SO YOU PLAN ON HITTING THEM IN THE VIRTUAL WORLD AND THE PHYSICAL WORLD.

"It's going to be a one-two punch." Cap flashed one of Stark's mischievous grins. "Please have the entire team assembled in the hangar in one hour."

As Coulson saluted his hero, Cap added, "And, Coulson? Thank you."

Inside the hangar, Captain America's team of **S.H.I.E.L.D.** agents and programmers were readying their equipment and suiting up for the battle as Fury watched from the sidelines.

"Welcome back, buddy," Falcon began. "Don't take this the wrong way, but are you sure you're up for this? No one would blame you if you sat this one out. Me and Nat can handle this."

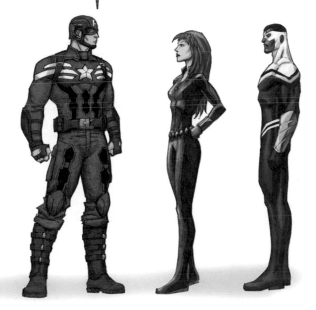

FALCON—SAM—I APPRECIATE YOUR CONCERN. BUT IF YOU'RE GOING AFTER HYDRA, I'M GOING WITH YOU.

"We're just concerned" Natasha said.

"I'm fine, Natasha. In fact, I'm better than fine. Now let's finish this briefing and get down to Liberty Island."

"What about your ride?" Falcon asked. "Do we still have to drag that old bike around?"

"Thanks for reminding me," Cap said. He took a small device out of one of the pouches on his belt and pressed down on its flat screen. There was a beeping sound, then a whirring, then a huge gust of wind. Everyone turned in amazement. The crowd of **S.H.I.E.L.D.** agents was speechless.

Fury looked at Captain America, totally shocked.

TWO WORDS...

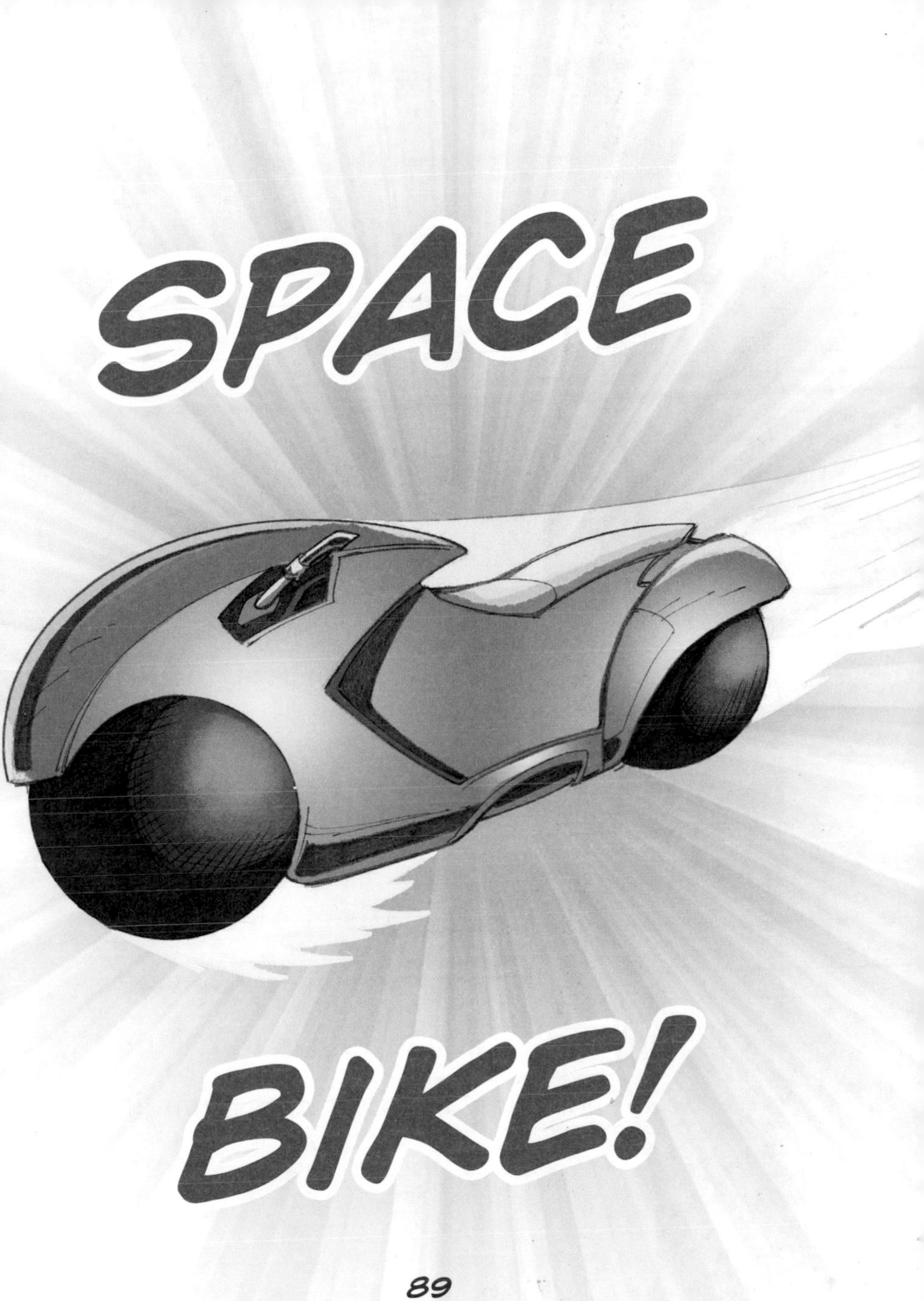
SPACE
BIKE!

CHAPTER
8

Captain America, Falcon, Black Widow, and their battalion of **S.H.I.E.L.D.** agents were hidden throughout Liberty Island, waiting for **HYDRA** to make its move.

Just as the sun was setting, they heard a low humming. They looked up to see giant zeppelins floating toward the Statue of Liberty. Then they heard loud splashing sounds and saw vehicles rising from the bay. The invasion had begun.

Cap signaled everyone to remain where they were. He wanted the battle contained to the island, so they would have to wait until *HYDRA* disembarked and made the first move. As if on cue, **Zola's** voice reverberated from the lead zeppelin.

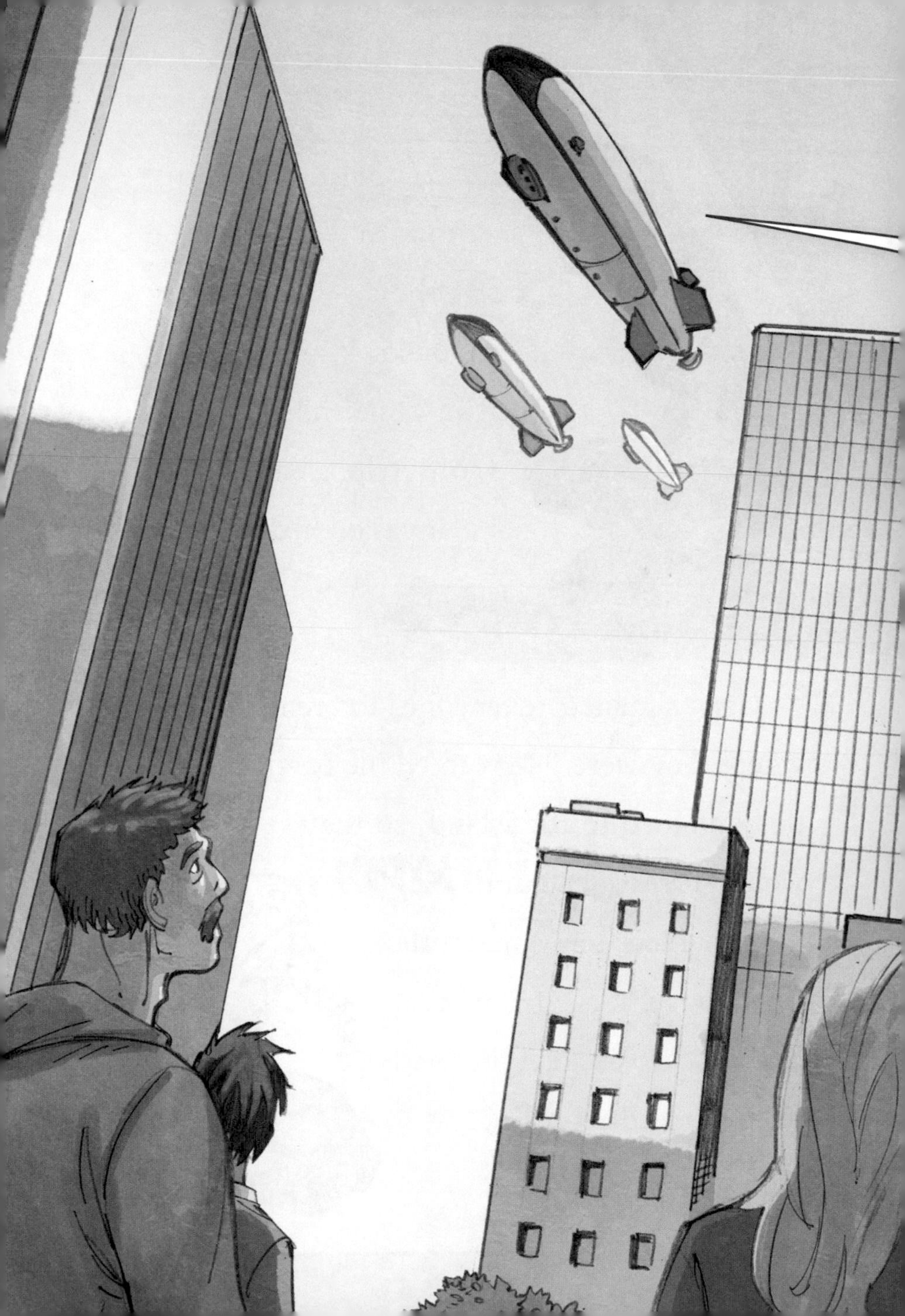

ATTENTION!
ATTENTION!

I, ARNIM ZOLA, LEADER OF HYDRA, NOW CONTROL ALL TRANSMISSIONS.

"I control all information! I control all of you! Today, the world will feel the unmatched power of **HYDRA.** For too long we have stayed hidden in the shadows. Now, we will rise. Now, **HYDRA** and its Tomorrow Army will take its rightful place at the head of the world."

In response, the **HYDRA** soldiers and the brainwashed Tomorrow Army threw their arms into the air and yelled, **"HAIL, HYDRA!"**

Cap gripped his shield and was ready to lead the attack when an eerie green wave of energy shot down from the zeppelin at the statue's crown.

The Statue of Liberty

"They're going to destroy the statue!" Falcon said in a hushed, urgent tone.

"No," Cap replied. "If they wanted to destroy it, they would've done that by now. Zola has something else in mind."

"Look!" Black Widow shouted. The beams Zola had fired made the statue glow. Then it looked as if the statue was melting. Then, slowly, the statue began to change its shape. "They're using matter reorganizers. Not even Stark has that technology!"

The heroes looked on in horror as parts of the statue transformed before their very eyes. Zola melted the statue's head and spiked crown, then fired the ray again and molded them into a hideous, many-tentacled skull, the very symbol of HYDRA.

"If you cut off one head, two more will grow! HAIL, HYDRA," Zola's voice then boomed from above.

Captain America stood horrified by this grotesque symbol of evil. For a split second, he felt utterly defeated. Then, as the last soldiers of the Tomorrow Army emerged from their vehicles and advanced on land, he felt a hand on his shoulder.

"Cap," Black Widow said softly. **"It's time."**

Cap felt hope return.

"Let's go," he said, swinging his shield around and charging toward the statue's base.

ZOLA, YOU
AND HYDRA HAVE
ONE CHANCE TO STAND
DOWN AND SURRENDER.
I WON'T ASK
AGAIN!

"Herr Captain, so soon recovered, I see," Zola said as he leaned out of the zeppelin's window and addressed the Super Hero. "Wunderbar. I had hoped you would attend the festivities and the invasion of your precious New York City." Zola pressed a button on his wrist gauntlet, and the Tomorrow Army's helmets flashed a brief red light. They had been upgraded with new instructions: commence the attack, and bring Captain America to Zola. The fight was on!

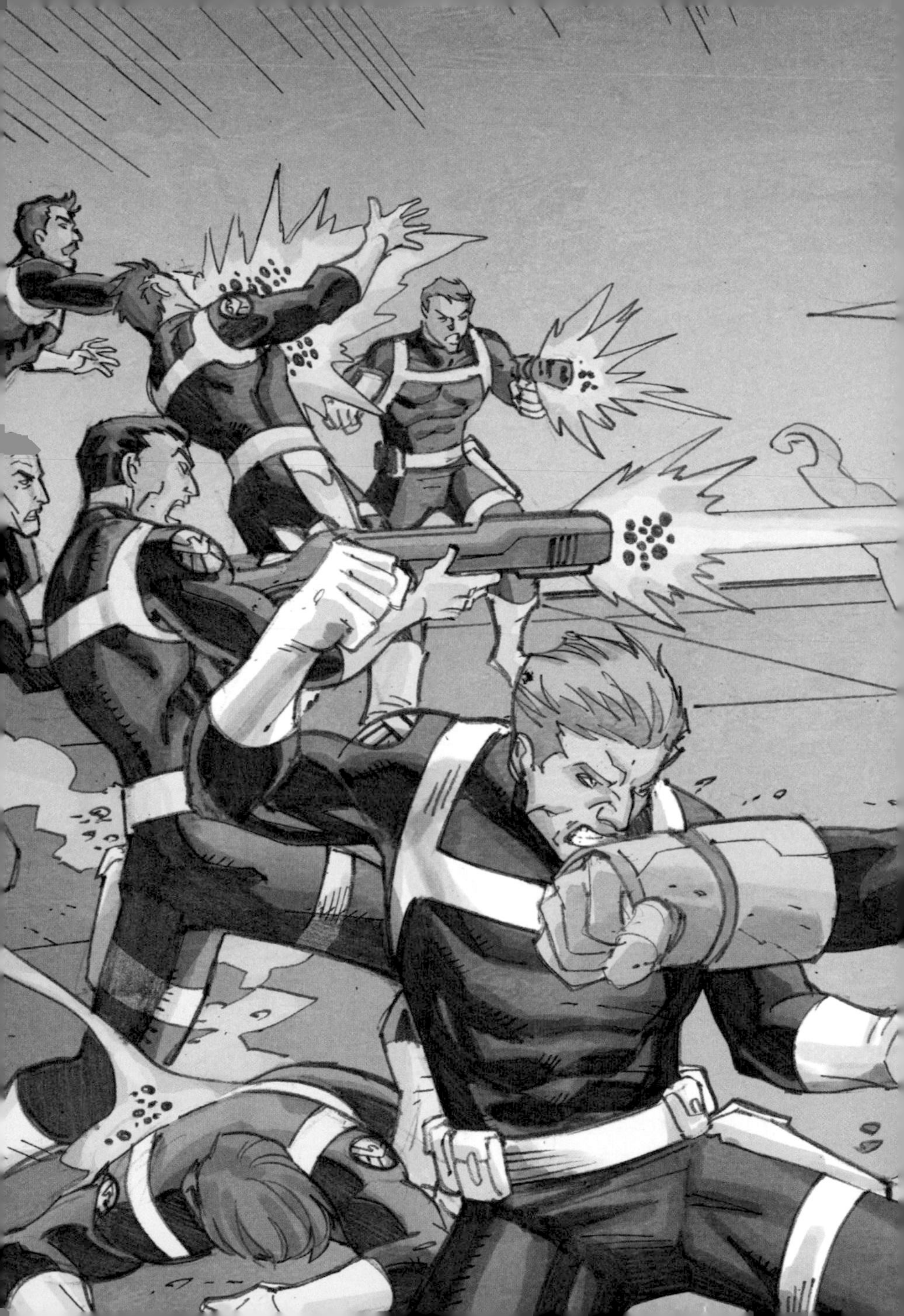

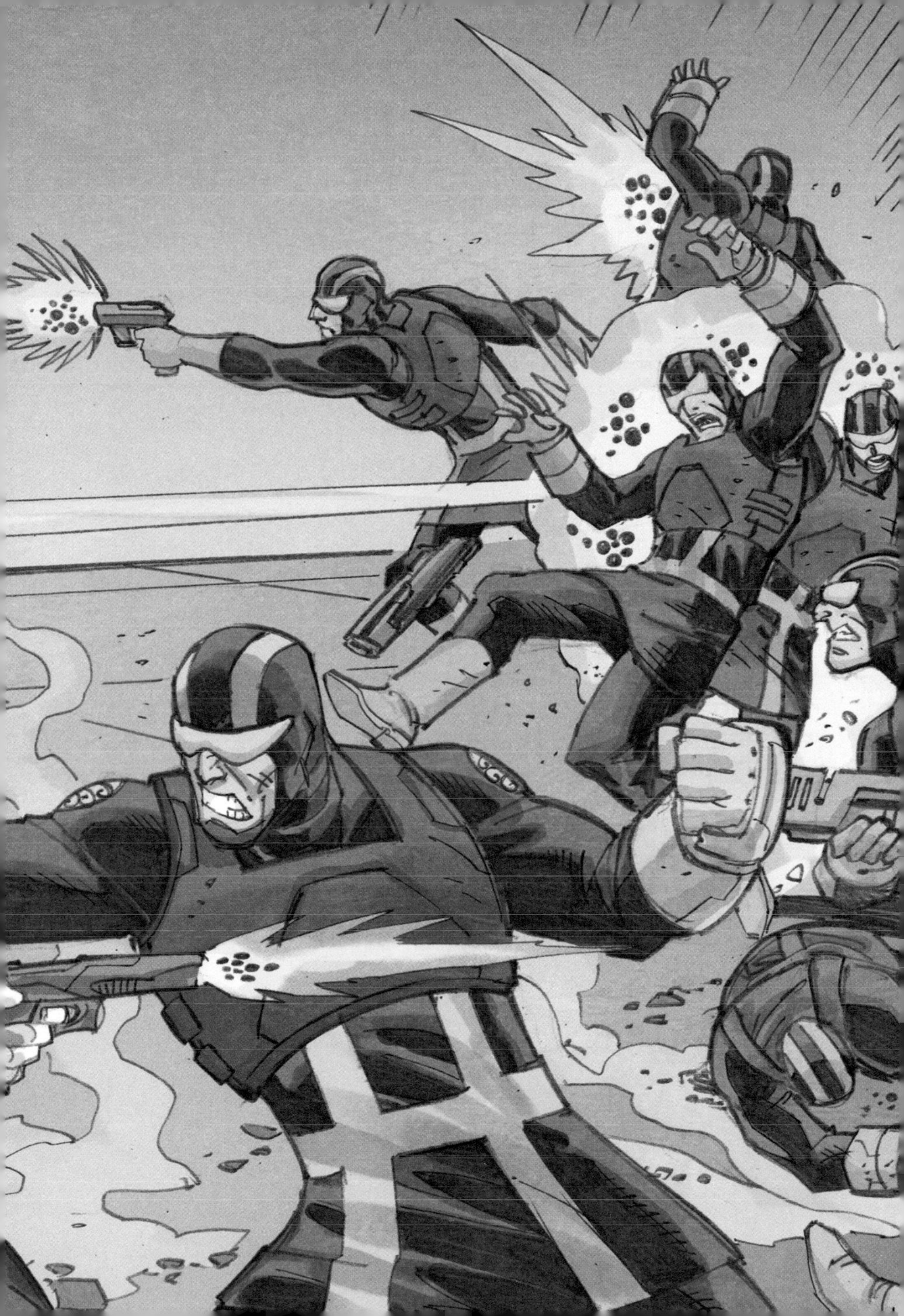

In mere minutes, it was clear that **HYDRA** had the upper hand.

Cap radioed the **S.H.I.E.L.D.** tech team stationed on a rooftop in lower Manhattan, led by Coulson. "Coulson, report! Any chance of jamming their communications systems, or knocking them out entirely?"

"We're working on it, sir," Coulson replied. "Their signals are being scrambled, and we've been unable to pinpoint their exact frequency. I need two more minutes."

"The battle might be over in two minutes," Cap yelled. **"You have one!"**

100

HUH?

Cap went back to the battle and threw his shield as hard as he could. It bounced off one, two, three Tomorrow Army helmets, momentarily knocking soldiers down.

Cap reached out to retrieve his shield, but it never returned. Instead, a bigger arm covered in wires and tech had the shield in its grasp. It was the original **HYDRA** super-agent.

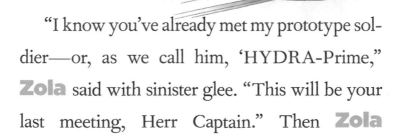

"I know you've already met my prototype soldier—or, as we call him, 'HYDRA-Prime," **Zola** said with sinister glee. "This will be your last meeting, Herr Captain." Then **Zola**

addressed HYDRA-Prime. **"Finish them,"** **Zola** commanded. HYDRA-Prime nodded and advanced toward Captain America.

"Didn't take my advice the first time we met, hmmm?" the villain asked as he threw Cap's shield to the ground.

"Bring it on, pal," Cap said through gritted teeth. It was time for a rematch!

CHAPTER 9

Captain America's fist slammed into HYDRA-Prime's jaw.

CRACK!

WHUMP!

HYDRA-Prime delivered a powerful kick to Cap's ribs. As the two men continued their knock-down, drag-out fight, **Arnim Zola** grabbed a rope and descended from his zeppelin onto the Statue of Liberty, where **HYDRA** agents were connecting the Techno-Disruptor to the opposite side of the transformed face. **Zola** cackled. "Soon Lady Liberty will be singing out of the other side of her mouth that I am her rightful leader!"

Back on the ground, Cap was out of breath and in pain. He had managed to grab his shield, but he was still losing. **"You are weak, Captain,"** HYDRA-Prime taunted. **"You cannot defeat me alone!"**

"You're so right," Cap said as he clicked on a small homing device from one of his pouches. "That's why I won't repeat the same mistake I made last time. This time I'm not alone!"

Within seconds, Falcon and Black Widow sprang into action. Falcon soared toward HYDRA-Prime as fast as he could, but HYDRA-Prime was faster.

OOMPH!

The two heroes **collided** and **fell** to the **ground.** HYDRA-Prime merely laughed. **"You will have to do better than that!"**

"Okay, how about this!" Cap said, landing a right hook across HYDRA-Prime's face. Cap quickly turned and regrouped with Falcon and Black Widow.

"You weren't kidding about this guy," Falcon said. "What's our plan?"

Before Cap answered, he hurled his shield at HYDRA-Prime. It smashed into his chest and returned to Cap. HYDRA-Prime staggered back and roared in pain. Captain America had bought them a few seconds of planning. **"I'm his main target,"** Cap said. "I'll provide cover; you two disable his tech—but do it quickly. I can't go another twelve rounds with this guy." Then Cap's eyes suddenly grew wide. *"THAT'S IT!"* he exclaimed. *"BOXING!"*

Black Widow and Falcon looked at him, confused.

"We have to go twelve rounds with him. He won't expect that. He's looking to end this quickly. We've got to fight him like Joe Louis would: methodical and controlled, over and over again."

"That's Joltin' Joe," Falcon quietly said to Black Widow.

"Joltin' Joe was a baseball player, genius, not a boxer," Black Widow corrected. **"Now look alive—here he comes!"**

The Super Villain charged toward them, then pointed his hands in their direction and fired bolts of electricity from his fingertips.

Cap raised his shield and deflected the bolts right back at the villain, temporarily distracting him. Falcon and Black Widow used the distraction to their advantage. Falcon fired his grappling hook and wrapped it around the villain's high-tech boots, tripping him up and sending him crashing to the ground.

As he fell, Black Widow fired her stingers

directly at the side of his helmet in hopes of damaging the wires that connected it to the chest piece.

HYDRA-Prime staggered again and was knocked back by a spinning red, white, and blue blur. As Black Widow and Falcon attacked from the side, Cap charged from the front. As they fought, each hero took a turn leading. When HYDRA-Prime turned to face one of them, the other two heroes would jump in. Falcon and Black Widow followed Cap's lead, and soon the three heroes were working in unison. Their attack was methodical and controlled, and they were wearing down HYDRA-Prime.

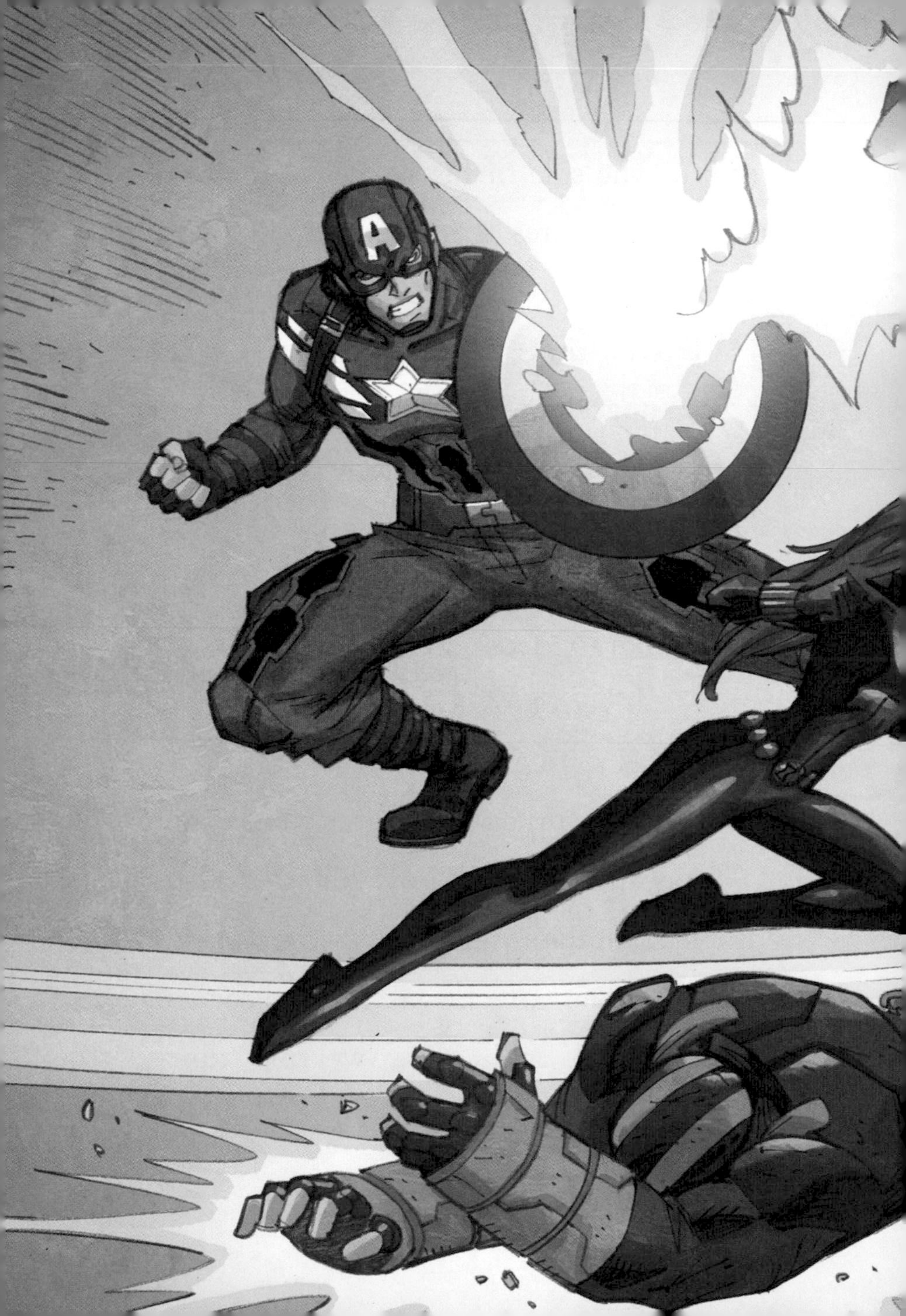

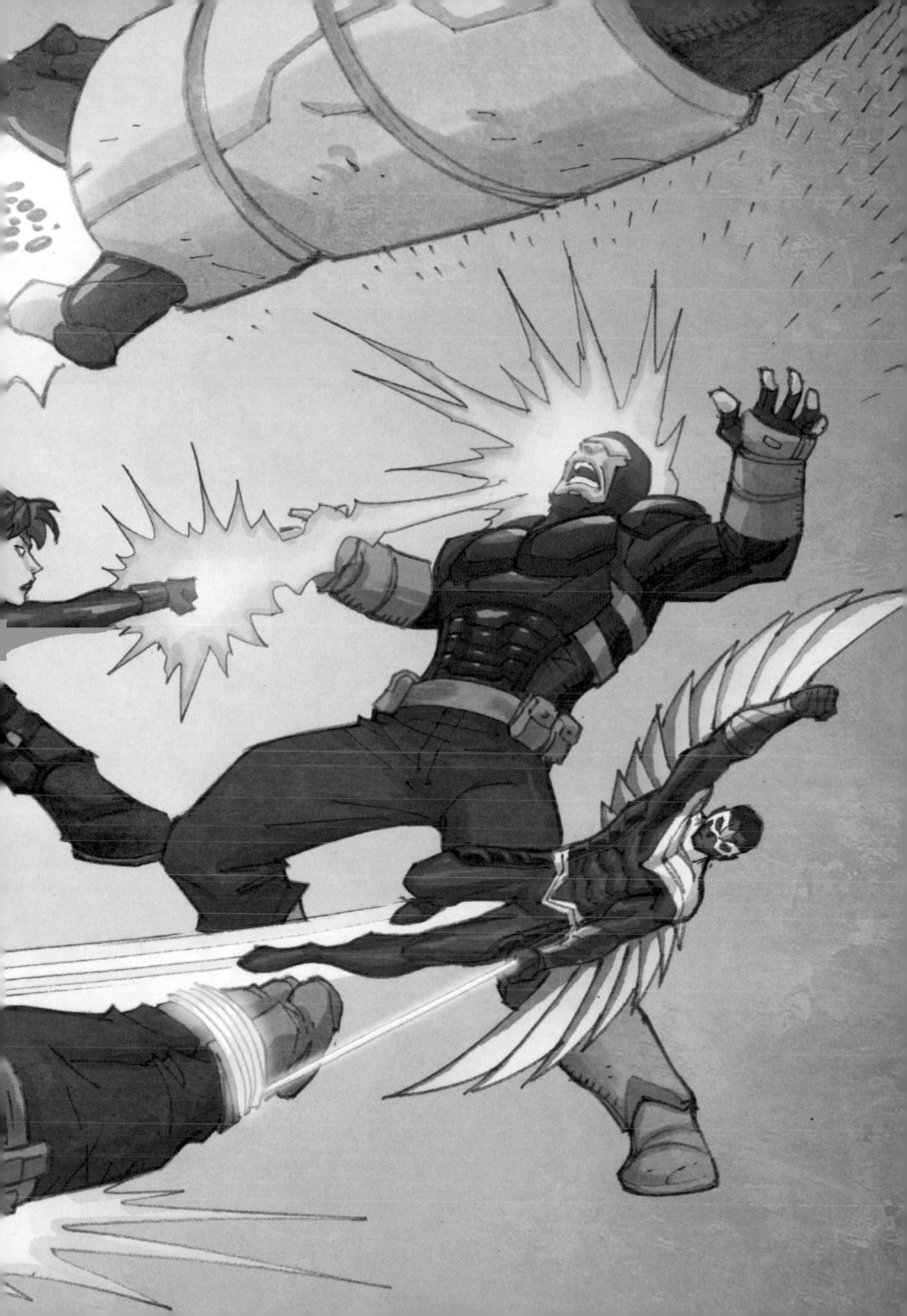

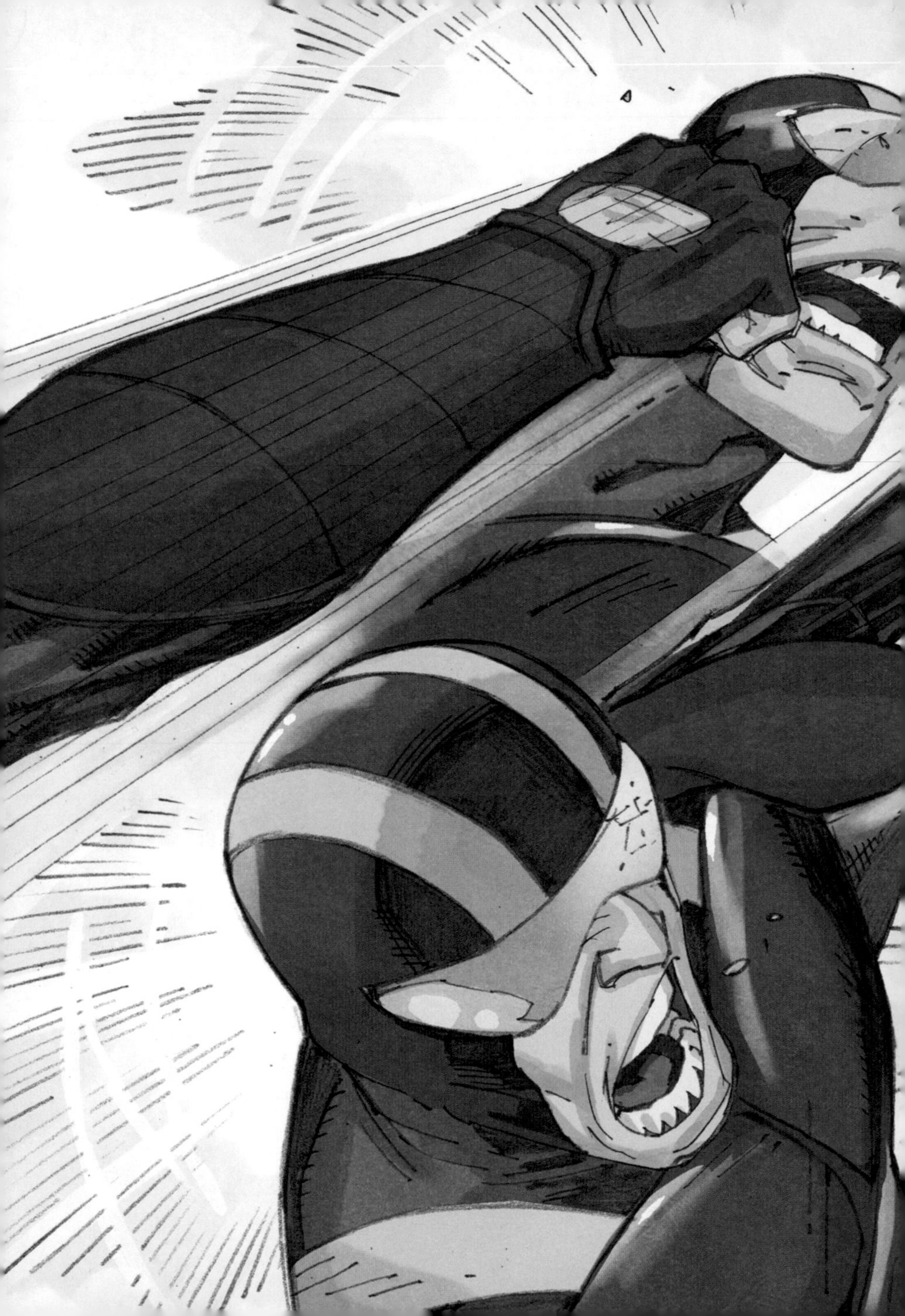

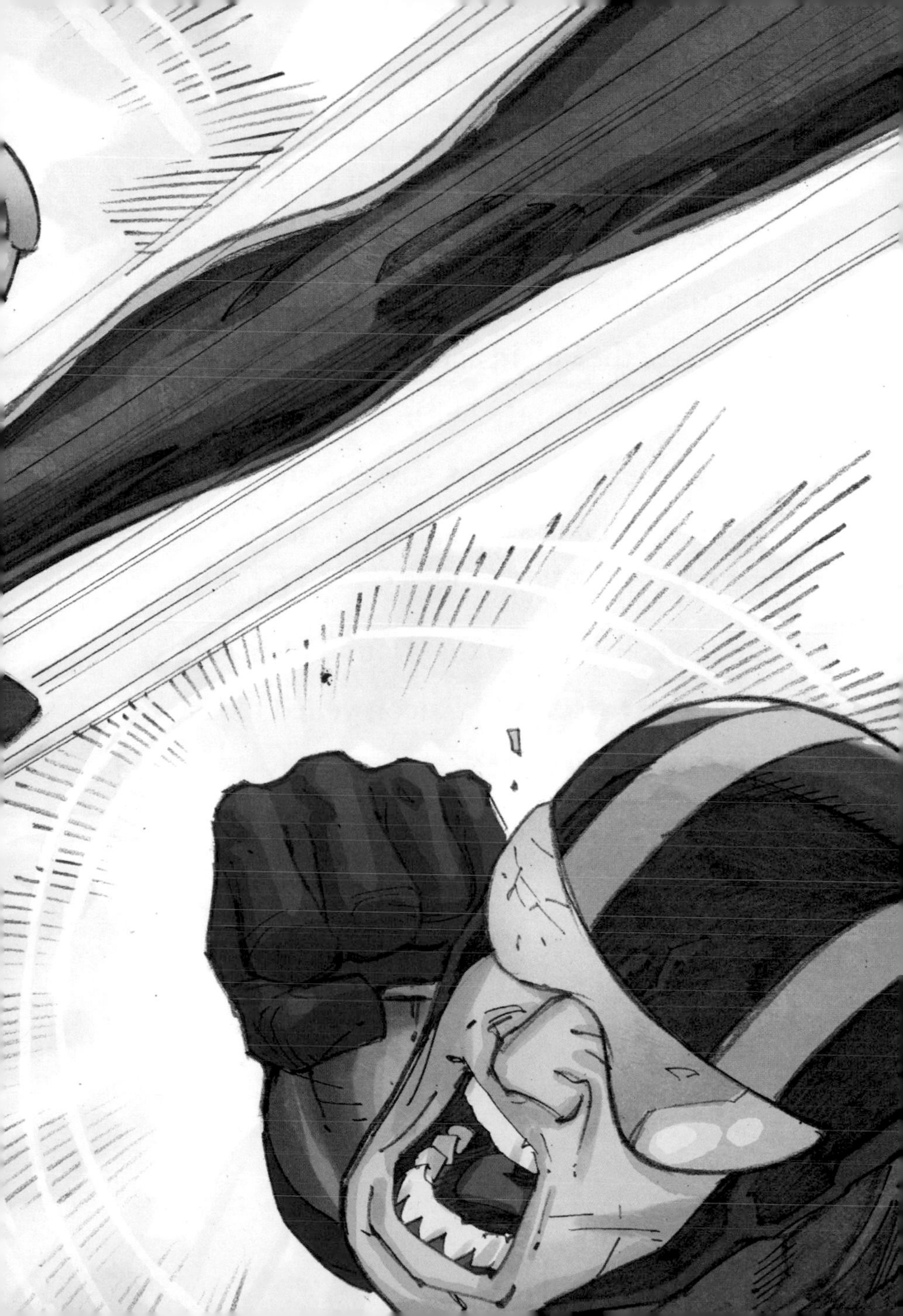

HYDRA-Prime lunged at Cap. The villain swung and missed, and Cap knew it was time for the final strike. Captain America jumped on top of the villain and grabbed the now damaged wires tightly with both hands. Then, using every ounce of strength in his Super-Soldier body, he ripped them out.

HYDRA-Prime let out a loud scream before collapsing to the ground, defeated.

"You did it!" Falcon yelled to Cap.

"We did it!" Cap quickly corrected.

"But it's not over yet. Zola's still standing. We have to stop him—and fast!"

"I can reach the top of the Statue of Liberty in twenty seconds," Falcon said as he began to extend his hard-light wings.

"Too slow!" Cap replied as he pressed a remote. His space bike streaked through the sky and then down toward the heroes. The First Avenger jumped in the air, grabbed the handlebars, and steered the bike straight up toward Zola.

As Cap approached the crown,

Zola quickly grabbed a gauntlet from one of his fallen Tomorrow Army soldiers and fired bolts of electricity toward Cap. Cap dove the flying motorcycle out of the way, then revved its engines and sped through an opening in the crown. He jumped off the hovering bike to face **Zola.**

"Once again, you are too late, Herr Captain. I have already won," **Zola** said as the Techno-Disruptor next to them sprang to life!

Just then, Cap heard a transmission from Coulson:

CAP—WE'VE FIGURED OUT HYDRA'S TECH! WE CAN SHUT IT DOWN AND DISABLE THE TOMORROW ARMY!

I HAVE ALREADY WON!

But energy waves had already begun to cascade from the device toward Manhattan. Slowly, all technology began to fail and shut down, including **S.H.I.E.L.D.'s** tech! Cap's flying motorcycle crashed to the ground with a loud **THUD**. He had to destroy the Techno-Disruptor—**now!**

Captain America advanced toward **Zola,** determined to stop him and the device. The villain cackled. "Fool! Your Super-Soldier strength is no match for my genius intellect! I control it all, Herr Captain! And he who controls technology controls the future!"

"And those who don't learn from the past are doomed to repeat it!" Cap replied. He grabbed **Zola** and lifted him high above his head, throwing the Hydra leader through the air.

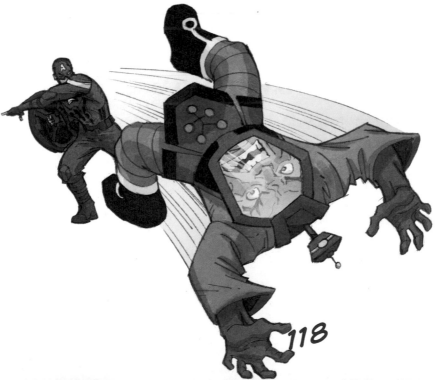

118

Zola landed with a *SMASH* and fell back, sliding out of the crown.

"Admirable, Herr Captain, but you have only slowed me down," the villain said.

Cap ignored him and flung his shield. It whizzed across the crown and landed with a **ZING** in the side of the Techno-Disruptor. The machine sputtered and sparked, but it wasn't enough to stop it. Cap pulled his shield from the machine and ran toward his space bike. "Guess we're going to have to do this the old-fashioned way."

Cap tried to activate the flying **motorcycle**  but it was no use. Thanks to the Techno-Disruptor, it had no power. But Cap just grinned and flipped a switch. Pieces of his bike flew through the air. Beneath the high-tech exterior was a fully functioning old-school motorcycle!

Cap grabbed a cable from the side of the

bike and
attached it
to the machine.
Then he jumped on
the starter and revved
the engine. Cap took a
deep breath and gunned
his bike, riding it—with
the machine attached—
straight off one of the
tentacles.

Cap—on the motor-
cycle with the machine still
attached—flew high into the
air, then started falling to the
island below.

It was Falcon! As he soared toward Cap, the
First Avenger jumped off the bike. Falcon
caught him just in time, and they flew high

into the air, the bike and the Techno-Disruptor exploding below!

The explosion was spectacular! Disabled by the **S.H.I.E.L.D.** team in lower Manhattan, the entire Tomorrow Army collapsed to the ground. When Coulson got the all clear from his men, he fired a single flare into the night: mission accomplished!

Somewhere along the East River, a New Yorker saw the explosion, then the flare, and decided to shoot his own fireworks into the sky. He was quickly joined by another New Yorker across town. And another. And another. And another.

Soon the sky was filled with explosions signifying the triumph of good over evil.

"'And the rockets' red glare, the bombs bursting in air,'" Cap said quietly to himself.

"We did it," Falcon said. "We stopped **HYDRA.**"

"And protected life, liberty, and the pursuit of happiness," Black Widow added.

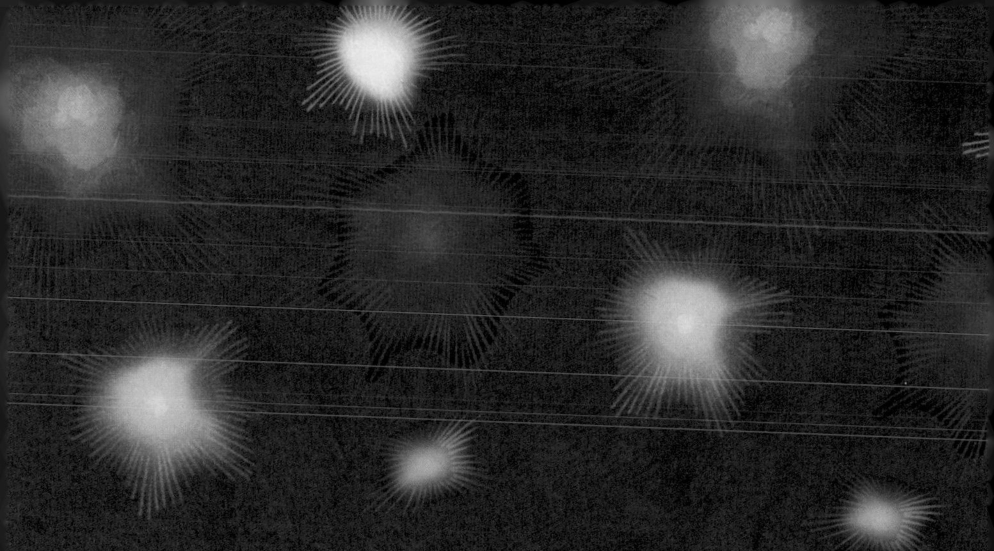

"Yes, but **Zola** got away," Cap said as he began to walk through the wreckage. "He's not here. And neither is HYDRA-Prime."

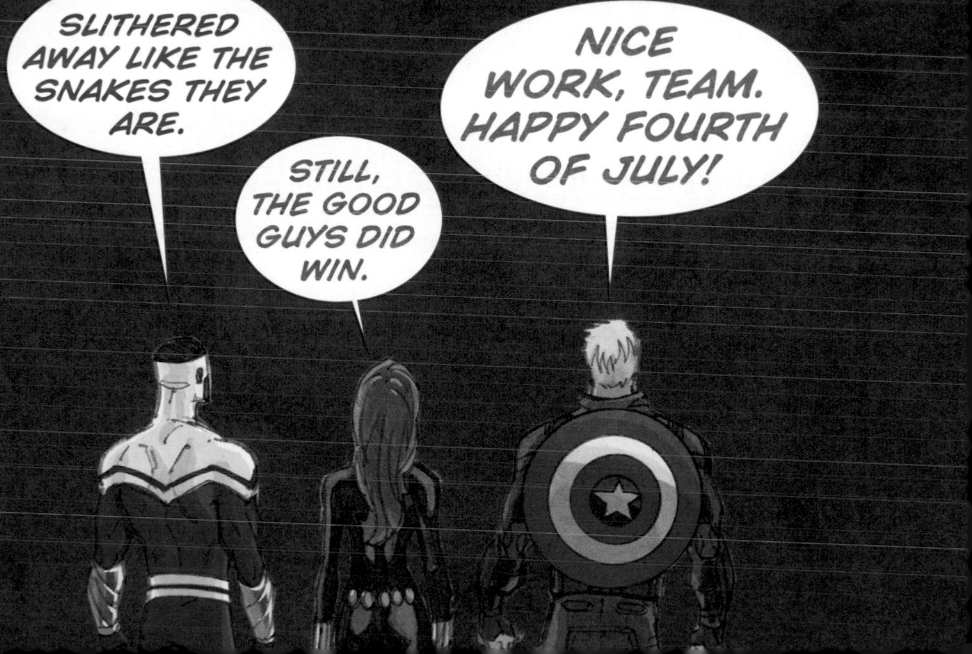
SLITHERED AWAY LIKE THE SNAKES THEY ARE.
STILL, THE GOOD GUYS DID WIN.
NICE WORK, TEAM. HAPPY FOURTH OF JULY!

CHAPTER 10

*T*he next morning, Steve Rogers woke up before his alarm. He got out of bed, stretched, and began his morning routine. He did his usual push-ups and sit-ups and soon began his morning run through Manhattan.

Steve's body ached from the battle the night before, but he was happy. He had saved the day. As he ran, he looked around Times Square. One of the giant screens was broadcasting familiar footage.

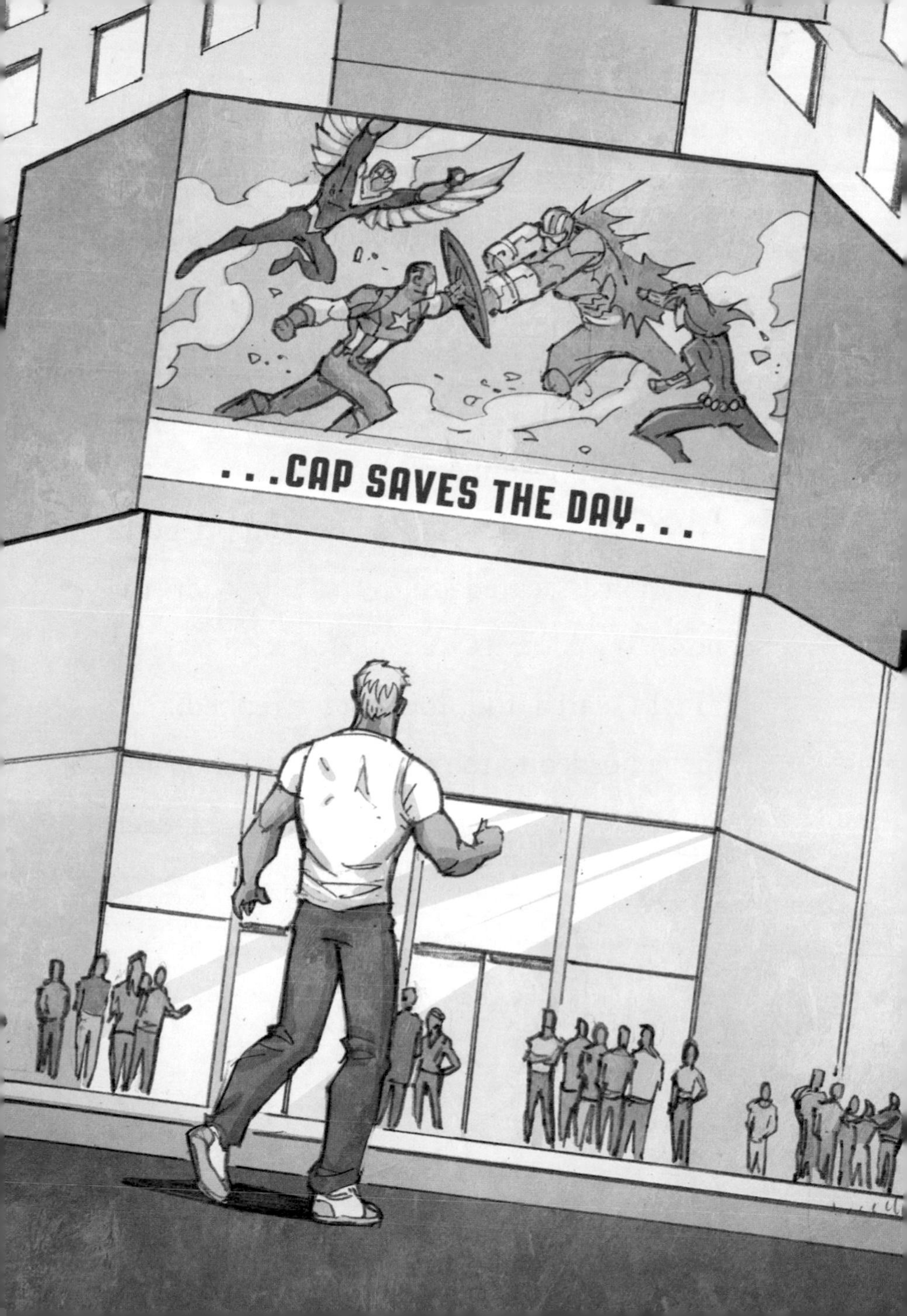
. . .CAP SAVES THE DAY. . .

The news anchor announced, "Captain America saves New York!"

He ran downtown and stopped by Old Joe's for his morning paper, smiling at the headline.

"NICE JOB," Old Joe said. "I gotta tell ya, I was scared until I saw you on the scene."

"I was scared, too, Joe," Steve replied.

Steve headed to the trendy coffee shop and went inside. Everyone was talking to each

other about what had happened the night before. Some were huddled around cell phones looking at pictures of the battle, and others were sitting at tables deep in conversation, but they were all connected—all bound by the same unbelievable events that had happened on the Fourth of July.

Steve stepped to the counter and saw the kid from the last time he had been there. Much to Steve's surprise, the kid remembered him. **"HEY, CUP OF JOE, BLACK, RIGHT?"** Steve nodded. "Coming right up, Cap!"

As Steve waited for his coffee, a few people came up and asked to take pictures. Others patted him on the back or shook his hand. After a few minutes, Steve paid for his coffee and sat on his usual bench outside. He looked across

the water at Liberty Island.
Construction crews were
already hard at work fixing
the statue. Scaffolding rose
as high as the crown.

Then Steve looked around. He saw kids pretending to be Super Heroes. A young couple were walking down the street holding hands, and he overheard them say how happy they were that Cap had saved the day. They didn't know that Captain America was sitting just a few feet from them. The city was bustling with energy, and all was right with the world.

Steve was happy to be alive. Thanks to the past few weeks, Steve had learned to appreciate what he had but also remember what had come before. He realized that he had to adapt with the times instead of living in the past. He also realized the importance of friends, and of working together and asking for help. Steve let out a contented sigh of relief. Then he heard a beeping sound.

Steve lifted the cell phone Tony Stark had given him and saw a text from Avengers Mansion. It read:

Steve tapped the screen and was soon staring at Sam Wilson's face on his phone. "What's the situation?" Steve asked.

"It's Batroc," Sam began. "You, me, and Natasha are back in action. And I think we're going to need the others."

Steve smiled. "Text me your coordinates, and tell the rest of the Avengers to stand by to assemble," he said.

"I'M ON MY WAY!"

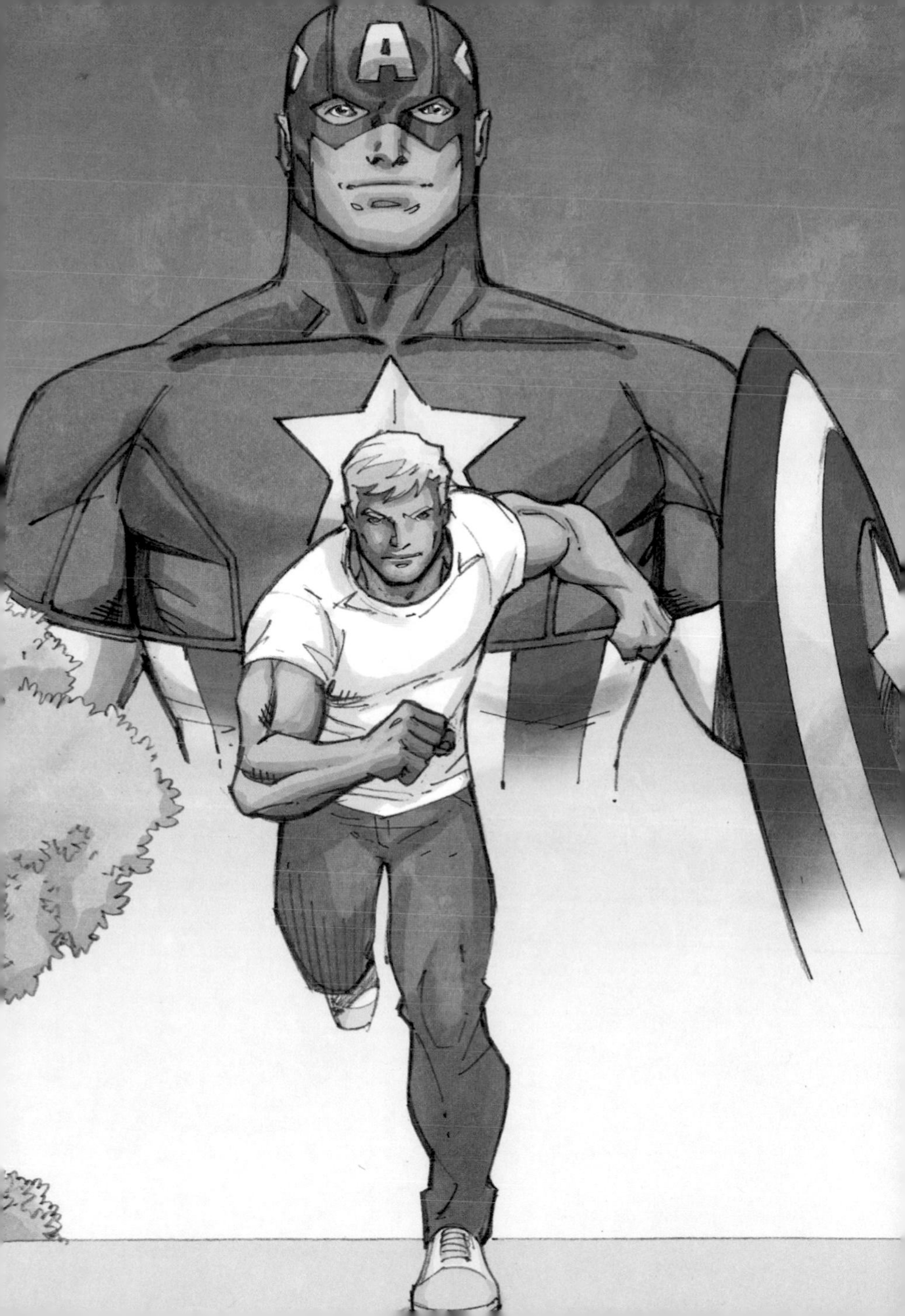